MORAINE'S EDGE
BOOKS

Rosette

A Novel of Pioneer Michigan

CINDY RINAMAN MARSCH

Illustrated by Betsy Marsch

This is a work of fiction based on historical facts, including an original journal and public records of birth, marriage, divorce, residence, property ownership, and burial. Some details and names have been conflated to unify the story.

Select details in this book have been confirmed or supplied by the work of William Robert Brittenham (deceased), *The Garter Family of New York and Michigan* (Poughkeepsie, NY: 2006), used by permission of his family.

Details of the school house come from George L. Jordan, "History of the Riker School District No. 9, Orange," unpublished manuscript presented at the Pioneer Day Celebration, March 29, 1940. Retyped 1989 by Ford Wright, used by permission.

Details of Abraham Lincoln's 1856 speech in Bronson Park, Kalamazoo, Michigan, are used by permission of the Kalamazoo Public Library.

Details of an apple-paring party are inspired by Mary E. Wilkins, "The Stockwells' Apple-Paring Bee," in *The Ladies' Home Journal*, XIV:11 (October 1897) .
http://wilkinsfreeman.info/Short/StockwellsApple-ParingBee.htm

First printed in the United States of America 2016
Print ISBN-10: 0-9971127-1-9
Print ISBN-13: 978-0-9971127-1-9

Moraine's Edge Books
154 Dight Road
Slippery Rock, PA 16057
MorainesEdgeBooks.com
info@MorainesEdgeBooks.com

Join the Readers List at RosetteBook.com to receive news and special offers on additional publications, including a transcription of Rosette's journal.

For Rosette,
who died unremarked
a century ago,
but whose words were
left for us.

Contents

Contents

PREFACE

*I*N IONIA COUNTY, MICHIGAN, in September of 1856, Rosette Cordelia Ramsdell, a 26-year-old schoolteacher and seamstress, daughter of Jacob and Sally, older sister of Solomon, Ellen, Jerome, and Frank, in earlier years bereaved of a sister Diana, began her fourteenth journal of her life. In gorgeous fine copperplate script now oxidized to brown, she numbered her pages and almost every day, told of the weather, the people, and the places in her life. We have temperature records and flood reports for one of the coldest winters on record in that area, election campaigning, an education conference featuring the now-famous John Milton Gregory (*The Seven Laws of Teaching*), and the work of a spiritualist medium.

In March 1858, she came to the last page, having in that book recorded her marriage to Otis Churchill on January 1, 1857, and the birth of their son DeWitt on September 6 of that year. These are the momentous events of the journal. But in between she records dreams, purchases, plantings and harvests, dances and myriad visits, maple sugar production, and the construction of a cutter (sleigh) for a honeymoon journey.

Preface

As I read and transcribed this journal of over 20,000 words, I was caught up in the history of Rosette and her family. I researched their gravestones and visited their farms in Michigan, still operating with owners and neighbors whose names appear on township plat maps going back over 150 years.

The Ramsdells were a distinguished family very active in education and politics. Rosette's brother Solomon was a bugler in the Union Army, imprisoned for a time at Andersonville. But Rosette and her husband Otis Churchill disappear to history, except for scraps. A government form records Otis filing for divorce in 1888. I have found a couple of letters Rosette wrote to the women's department of a national magazine in the 1890s. One newspaper reports a substantial inheritance Rosette received while living in Fargo, North Dakota in 1902, at age 72. And their son DeWitt's gravestone is in Fargo, dated 1913.

Rosette, a profoundly literate young woman, uses the language of her education and popular novels she read, crafting beautiful turns of phrase to share delightful episodes of her life. Much is veiled—we do not know she is betrothed to Otis until their wedding day. But tracing back through earlier entries, we see that some of her sewing projects were included in her trousseau. She does not write of her pregnancy until the night she refers to her "cholic" and the summoning of her mother and a doctor who arrives a couple of hours after the birth. She says little of her affection for Otis, though she does refer to difficulties with her emotions. Naively she relates dreams our generation immediately recognizes the significance of, without herself seeming to understand them.

And in one amazing twist, the journal entry on her wedding day formally praising the worth of her groom is later edited in pencil—and not in Otis's favor.

Rosette fascinated me, and I transcribed the last page of her journal with a pang. I have eagerly researched her

Preface

life and the lives of the people around her. When I stood on the property of the families' farms and gazed about at the abundant Michigan summer, the fields now tilled with modern equipment but layered over with centuries-old ways as well, I felt grounded in her world, even more than through her journal.

I believe Rosette deserves a wider circle of friends, so I present this story, consistent with her journal and containing much language from it. The italicized portions are transcribed or slightly edited from the journal, and elsewhere in the story I borrow language from the journal without indicating so. Rosette's true story is within and beyond the journal. Where I do not have the facts I have invented likely ones. I hope the result is faithful to the real Rosette, her family, and their friends. If I misrepresent them, it is only because I have not yet come to know them well enough.

Cindy Rinaman Marsch
December 2015

1888 DAKOTA

TERRITORY

Rosette - Dissolution

TILL QUICK AND SLIM, still well turned out at fifty-eight. With shine to my hair—when I can dress it—and light in my eyes. But suddenly cut off, with the flourish of a pen, the run of a press. I sit here still, in this dark sod shanty, my granddaughter outside chattering, her mother Lillie dragging the dusty wash off the line. We've scraped the earth—or my son DeWitt has—and we women have tended the children and labored long days to feed us all. In the quiet the babe is asleep in the cradle beside me, in the spot where the sunshine pries through—and the wind in winter. A generation ago DeWitt was the babe in my lap— and his father Otis chopping trees to clear the farm near my folks in Michigan. Now my son breaks the bones of the earth to farm here—to coax food from the soil and beat back the vermin that race us to harvest.

That little waver of afternoon sun flickers down on the letter in my lap. It's just a line or two from daughter Ella, folded round the notice in the newspaper. Otis has sued divorce on me. Two years' absence and I have deserted him, the law says. So be it—I will not answer for it.

I rode the train here two years ago, rumbling out west, then north, to whatever might be here for me, for my eldest son's family. A young family ought to have help from their folks in homesteading, as ours helped us. And so I came.

But, truth be told, moreso I left. I left what had long since shriveled and died. I left the oppressive eye of Otis's old mother waiting to be served and watching to quaver at me. I left Otis's deranged brother drooling and wild-eyed, gaining strength in middle-age. And I left my last babe, Percy—twelve then, fourteen now—who sees no wrong in Otis. So it is with the boys—they see their father's muscled arms and callused, scarred hands. The gleam in his eyes they mistake as ambition for the farm. Always something new he longs for, and better—better than I, for certain.

Most sad of all, I left the girls to the daily care of that menagerie. Ella writes of her suitor, and soon will fly into his arms. Her sisters have yet a few years. Among them they can keep the house, their routines set. The rhythms of the harvests will well enough provide for them all. I am grown too old—no matter I can still turn a reel at a dance—to bear it any longer.

I consider things this late afternoon, the sun slanting now against my heart. It beats a little chill, uncertain. I've been here two years, but I still do not know my place. What is this land? The lakes of nearby Eden—wishful name!—do provide for some game and water, but naked we are on this vast plain. We were snug enough in the sod house these two terrible winters, with just one little one, and another soon to be born. So it is every winter here, they say. Privations of one sort or another seem to find me, however much I devise against them.

Thirty-odd years ago it seemed enough to blaze our life together in the rich land of Michigan. Oh, how I long for our trees—the fruit and sugar and lumber without end. Out here the settlers plant what they hope will become fortresses against the wind, but in these settling years they are but twigs. There we had to pull down the trees to live, and here we have to raise them up, and hunker down in the meantime.

How drawn my daughter-in-law Lillie is here—pale after the babies, and another already on the way for next spring. DeWitt flames up somewhat like his father, but without the pith to answer this grassy land. He grinds his teeth in the night, as he has always fretted against what is. All around us others have given up, going home on the train, bedraggled and thin. We all brought promises with us, though mine in middle-age were wry. My one trunk held two bed-covers from early years—spades and love-knot designs—and a hat or two, with the odd feather. And I brought my pens and ink and that one journal out of dozens—the one from the year of our marriage and DeWitt's birth—to share with his family. I used to read bits of my journal to my brothers and sisters, my mother, my husband. And Otis read adventure tales to me and even to DeWitt as a young boy . . .

But our time for reading here has been lost in cares, or we find no heart left for it when time is right—when we are crowded in upon one another in this small place.

I turn to the page from that day:

> *Thursday January 1st. 1857. Another new year. And the day was a beautiful one, & one that will be remembered by me as being the happiest in my life; as I was joined in the holy & happy bonds of marriage with the man, whom above all the earth I sincerely love & respect. That man is Otis Churchill.*

A tear at that, for what I've lost, when I thought bitterness had dried them all away.

I do not keep a journal now. The small ink supply I came with is gone, and much else calls for the money. I keep some pencils for when I needs must write a line or two. Now, this day with the news, I must tell the truth my two years' sojourn has already told. And so the pencil strikes through "happiest" and stops.

A day to remember indeed, and even days of joy to follow, though set upon and finally swallowed up. I add a prefix here and here, then line out what my bride-self wrote to replace the words with what is, and has always been, though I did not know it then:

*I was joined in the **UN**holy & **UN**happy bonds of marriage with the man, whom above all the earth I sincerely ~~love & respect~~ **DETEST & ABHOR**. That man is Otis Churchill.*

1856 MICHIGAN

Monday 8th. The three Professors instructed us by turns. The studies presented were arithmetic, bookkeeping, elocution, &c. . . . The evening was a beautiful one, the moon shining brightly. Mr. [Fox] has a very pleasant family, & is a gentleman himself. They have a melodean & accordeon here & music, combined with happy dispositions [that] make theirs a pleasant & happy home.

Thursday 18th. Mrs. B. was quilting. We all went to work & got it off about 9 o'clock I guess. . . . It is pleasant to be alone sometimes. We are free to act as we choose, having none but the Allseeing eye to spy our actions. I am now writing seated on a log, being on my way across the river. It is a pleasant, warm day, but the wind blows cool. Now my thoughts are calm and peaceful & then they are torn by contending emotions. But I am learning severe & profitable lessons, & by the help of God I will not complain. I am striving to do better, & upward & onward must be my course. The guilty conscience is its own accuser, & the wicked will be punished sooner or later.

Solomon - Town

HE WAGON JERKED AND RUMBLED along the ruts that we'll soon build into a road out to our place from town, through the woods we're clearing this year. So far it's just our folks doing the work, but that makes it ours. As the eldest son of Jacob Ramsdell, my part today is to fetch my sister after her week at the Teachers' Institute.

Since 1835, when Rosette was five and I a babe, we've been here in Michigan, come out from New York. Before that our grandparents—Ramsdells and Richardsons— came to New York from Massachusetts, and their folks to Massachusetts from England long ago. When I was just thirteen we came to Ionia County from Kalamazoo and began to build the house and barn on Dad's place. Now we are waiting for Rosette to marry one day. And as she tarries with that, I have bought adjoining land to start my own farm and bring a wife to it—whoever she may be.

My father has a grand plan for us, and I have made it my own, doing what he would have me do and liking it. He is a wise man, and good—a just-graying patriarch on the model of Isaac or Jacob. He has a sense of history and prophecy to lead him and sees us filling this land with our own families and like-minded neighbors. He presides at table with local dignitaries, or makes envoys to neighboring towns, reaching his influence through the countryside as he once laid out the streets for Kalamazoo.

All his life Father has gathered property and knowledge to himself, but not hoarded it. He welcomes new neighbors and offers skill to those who want to learn. I double his production as I match his ways, overmatching his strength and stamina now. I even begin to gain my own authority with those around us. Only Myron King, south of us, with his own one-hundred sixty acres, has such success as does the Ramsdell enterprise.

I may be young, but I see my way—his way—is a good one. By my age Father already had a wife and child, and I am eager for my own. When I walk the wagon tracks near our place I spy out this or that plat and consider—yes, that's a good one. No, that one floods and the soil is sandy. I want to take the best of what Father has taught me and then add my own ways to it. But I am content now to watch and wait for just the right girl.

Rosette has gone forth as a teacher, to play out Father's education ideals or follow those of others he thinks worthy. I drove her in our wagon last week for the Teachers' Institute in Lyons, where I was to play fiddle at the hotel that night. But we almost failed to arrive. With the bridge out we were obliged to ford the river there. The horse, Bruno, shied as we entered, rearing back and thrashing so that we were nearly thrown out. He broke the forward end board and whippletree—at least, that was all I could see at the time.

Rosette jumped out of her own accord, and several nearby fellows came to our aid. The things in the wagon— our bags, some maps of hers, and my fiddle—were kept safe, though I hate to think what could have happened to them if we had overturned. "No matter!" Rosette cried, her skirts dragging wet from her landing just at the edge of the water. But my sister, alone among all the ladies we know, wears short skirts and bloomers, she calls them, and the costume proved handy that day. She waved me off to see to the wagon—"I shall soon enough be in dry things." She matter-of-factly climbed the bank by where the wagon fetched up, then began to shed her boots and squeeze her clothing dry.

I let myself down into the waist-high water and calmed Bruno, stroking his neck and murmuring to him, both of us soaked. "What a nice fix you've gotten us into now!" I chided him. I looked again to Rosette and saw as she slipped her bare feet into her sodden boots, took up her maps and bag, and began to walk the small distance from there.

Our old friend Luther Smith was one of the men who helped, and together we got Bruno up the bank on the homeward side. We inspected the damage, and I knew it was more than I could handle before I had to be at the hotel. Repairs would have to wait.

"Well, Solomon," Luther said, "I'd be pleased to take Bruno to my place to stable him until tomorrow."

"That would be a kindness," I answered.

"And I'll stable you, too, if you can make your way along the river yourself after you play tonight," he said with a grin.

"Or," I replied, "You can come to the hotel and let my fiddle pay for my keep."

"And lead you back, to make sure you don't lose your way," he said.

"—And make sure I don't lose my way."

We secured the wagon and walked Bruno along the course of the river north and east, toward Montrose, along the rise over the steep riverbank. We were quiet, remembering our many woods walks in our growing-up years—he silently pointed out the tree still bearing our old rope. We used to tag along to town with Father and disappear to our swinging tree when the water was high, letting loose to fall yelling into the rippling current.

I cleaned myself up at Luther's shanty he's setting up for a farm nicely situated in a bend of the river above the mill—safe even when it floods. Then I made my own way into Lyons with my fiddle for my engagement.

It's becoming a fine town—fresh hammering and painting build out from the center every time I come in from the farm. Main Street with the bank and the hotel and other shops, and around the corner, other places of business. The Institute would board the teachers in various homes, as they are used to, and save the expense of the hotel. I wondered where Rosette would stay, but I knew she would tell me all when she came home the next week.

I climbed the steps to the Pacific Hotel. Only a half-dozen were there having dinner, but with white tablecloths and a waiter. I found my spot in the corner and unlatched the case, and two diners looked up. What would they want? A scherzo, a Foster, a hymn? Both were strangers to me, but we have many strangers these days, the population of Ionia County tripling in a decade. If I gathered correctly, they might be professors with the Institute. So a scherzo. But first a mellow hymn to lead the mood.

As I played, one leaned toward the other to speak over my music, but the other nodded and turned partway toward me. When I finished playing, the two men waited until I was in the midst of my next piece, a little folk waltz, and took their leave. A young couple tapped their feet to the music, and I played more of that sort until Luther and some other men came in to hear. Then I began with the lively jigs the country people favor.

Late in the evening the diners faded out the door, and Luther and I made our way back to his place. We talked men's talk of the river and the town and livestock. In years past we might have talked boys' talk of—well, of the river and the town and livestock!

I managed to fix the wagon early next morning and got it back home for our work of the day. I stayed on the farm for the week, until time to fetch Rosette again at the close of the Institute. She intended to walk the seven miles, as we agreed even before the accident. But Luther has invited us both to spend the evening at his little shanty with some others, so I mean to meet her with the wagon.

* * *

I was just a mile from Lyons when I saw her, satchel on her arm, walking well toward home. She started at seeing me, then regained her stride before smiling a greeting and holding up her bag with her head cocked to the side. I climbed down and helped her up, which we would never have done at home. Town ways.

"I see you've got the wagon fixed, and Bruno settled again."

"Yes. Luther helped with tools, but that beast didn't want to see the river again twice in a week! How have you fared, Sister?" I guided the horse to continue toward Luther's instead of home, but Rosette did not notice. I wondered when she would.

"Just as I left town I tussled with a little war-like dog!" she laughed. "Have you ever seen him? He chooses a victim, it seems, almost every hour. He challenged me with a bark and pulled at my skirts, then trotted off so dignified." She paused, to better supply my curiosity. "There were such a lot of things to think about, a whole world of ideas at the Institute. Fine and noble ideas. The two professors dined at Mr. Fox's yesterday, and I asked a question."

"So you spoke to them? I think I played for them last week. And why were you at Fox's? I don't know about him.

..." I thought of him sidling up to young ladies. I don't like to think of him keeping boarders.

"Yes, I spoke to Professor Gregory, and he was gracious in his reply. I'll tell about Fox's in a moment—" she added. "Professor Gregory's text for Sunday was, 'Children are an inheritance from Heaven.' He said he thought perhaps it came from the Psalms."

"Something of that sort." I flicked the leads and clucked to urge Bruno on. Surely John Milton Gregory had deeper things to remark than that. But once Rosette sees a bright bird of an idea, she chases it without thought of the whole of the wood.

"Wait!" she cried. "I forgot! I need my maps. I engaged with Mr. Crampton to varnish them." We had all admired the maps Father brought from Kalamazoo for Rosette's teaching—Michigan, New York, and the World.

"Oh, why couldn't you remember before we got this far?" I cut the horse back around to face toward town again.

"And why were we going that way, Sol? Home is the other way."

"I wondered when you would notice that," I smiled. "Just be patient, and you will see." We doubled back, crossed the repaired bridge, and soon found ourselves in front of the Pacific Hotel. I drove down to Crampton's and she jumped down from the wagon, forgetting her town manners in her rush, and popped into his door. A few minutes later she shouldered her way out with her three rolled maps.

"Now what were we talking of before?" she asked as she climbed back up and tucked the maps under her skirts between us.

"Professor Gregory, and children, I believe."

"Yes. I asked whether perhaps children were a treasure for all and not just for their own parents. I could feel my cheeks flame with fright and feared they all saw it. But he approved of my question. He said that yes, our education of them must be like caring for treasured goods from our ancestors. They will make our future."

"Very fine. But surely you had some fun times, too." We put town behind us and bumped down toward the river.

"Well, of course I saw Martha, and met some others at Fox's. We could have used your fiddle, though he played melodeon and accordion. Such fun. And such a dream I had there!"

"Oh, your dreams. Of course. Tell me this one, and then we'll talk of the Institute."

"Well," she answered, "I'll read it to you from my journal."

"You've just started a new one, haven't you?" She pulled out the marbled brown book from the satchel at her feet. My sister has been filling journals like this one since she was a young girl. Her ink pot and pens are always in perfect order whenever someone comes out of the woods needing them for some note or other. Many of the settlers have but shanties, but nevertheless do business in full legal order. They make promissory notes and appeals to law to dignify what might be fistfights and crop-burning in a less civilized place. "What number is this?"

"Fourteen," she said. "And I started this one last week. I wonder how far it will go, and what will happen in those pages." She fanned the clean, ruled leaves, only the first few covered in her feathery hand. "My life has not been so eventful, but I keep finding things to write about. What do you think will fill this one? The last ones have Kalamazoo, and my school here. And what I thought was to be my marriage . . . Painful things—I almost wish I hadn't written my hopes."

She opened to the second page. "But here's my dream, then:

I dreamed that I was staying at Mr. Fox's and doing somewhat ill while there. He was determined to give me some medicine. He finally persuaded me to take some liquid, out of a tea-spoon which he held for me. I afterwards repented and told him I thought he had done very wrong, and myself too.

"What do you make of that?" she asked.

"I don't like it, is what I make of it. You didn't take any medicine or drink from him, did you? And surely he wasn't in your room?!"

"Oh no! I did meet him in the hall while I was in my dressing gown and cap, but his daughter-in-law was with me then. And in the evening we sang this song I copied from their Sanders' *Fourth Reader*. Here's a part of it . . ." She turned the page as we began bumping past the road onto the wagon track near the river ford, on our way to Luther's.

I love to look on a scene like this,
Of wild and carefree play,
And persuade myself that I am not old,
And my looks are not yet gray.
For it stirs the blood in an old man's heart;
And makes his pulses fly,
To catch the thrill of a happy voice,
And the light of a pleasant eye.

"I daresay you caught old Fox's eye," I grumbled.

"Oh, Sol, he means no harm, and we were in good company, altogether proper." She closed her book and slipped it into her bag. I left her to her faraway look and considered why I was so sharp with her—well, because she hasn't much wisdom. She needs an anchor, and then I would not fret about Fox and others like him. Well, not so much.

"But Professor Gregory?" I asked, breaking her quiet. "First, what is he like? I thought I might have seen him when I played at the hotel the other night. Father says he is becoming an important leader in education."

"Yes, you said that about playing for him. John Milton Gregory—such a name! He had beautiful manners, and a commanding voice. When he left he smiled at me in a telling way, to approve my words, I hope. But the young ladies were neat and well-spoken. I found I was able to be so much like them I hardly knew myself."

"Soon it will be the old life back at home, though."

"And where are we going, after all?" she asked, looking around at nothing but trees closing in on the track.

"Our dear Mr. Luther Smith has invited us to take our supper with him. And I did not think you would refuse a country evening, even after your elevated sojourn in Lyons."

"The town isn't so fine as all that, though, you know," she scolded. "I'm glad we are going to Luther's. Like old times. But I just remembered—" she caught herself. "I started at Mr. Hubbel's to board, with another teacher, and they have a parrot that talks almost like a human." She stuck her head over in front of me and wrinkled up her nose to whine, "'Polly wants a supper, Polly wants a supper!'"

I laughed as she wanted me to and asked, "So how came you to Fox's, then? You started at Hubbel's?"

"On the second day Hubbel said he could no longer keep me, so the Institute sent me to Fox instead."

"Well, if Professor Gregory and others were there, they must be keeping a good place."

"Yes," she sighed. "And Professor Gregory was not the only one—the other lecturers were fine as well. But I was terrified when they told us we would be writing a composition to present at the close! I've never written one in my life!"

"For all you've read them, though," I said.

"Well, of course, and mine is no matter. But Miss Gower's—oh, how lovely!"

"The principal teacher of the Union School should have an exemplary piece, I should think."

"Sometimes I despair of ever approaching what she is," she sighed.

"You do well enough—else the schools would not call on you to teach." I pulled back on the reins as Bruno picked his way over the rough ground.

Luther was finishing his milking as we arrived. After we climbed down from the wagon, he handed me the pail for a supper he laid on a board across the back of his goat cart. "Pleased to see you, Miss Ramsdell. I am honored to entertain you and your distinguished brother with this simple repast." He indicated his spread of a bowl of raspberries, a plate of pancakes, and some boiled eggs.

"We are honored beyond measure," Rosette replied, taking up his antique courtesy, and extending her hand to his bow for a mock kiss. We were suddenly back in childhood with a beloved playmate. When he lived with his father, the three of us would scamper off to the creek when we could. Luther dreaded his father, and when he could escape their place we'd find him on ours. I don't know how such a noble young man could come of a scoundrel like Frog Smith, but each man must make his own way. And Father and Mother gladly folded Luther into our family when he appeared among us.

I once thought Luther could be a good husband for Rosette. And so he could. But she—however much she humors him—doesn't think much of goats and a riverside shanty, unless it has a prosperous mill attached. And Luther is really a brother to us both.

He unhitched Bruno and led him to a bit of pasture the goat had not yet taken. At sunset we welcomed other friends who came through the woods to join us—Amos

Utter and his betrothed, Nancy, and my luckless friend
Cornelius McKelvey, who stumbles and breaks things and
manages nevertheless to keep his farm together. These
and a few others formed our company. The ladies
applauded when I fetched my fiddle, and they danced
with the men and twirled their skirts coyly among the few
remaining fireflies. Nancy cast adoring looks at Amos in
the firelight as I sawed away. Luther pranced about as
master of ceremonies, banging on any old thing to keep
time.

Rosette took part but held herself aloof, in all her tiny
dignity a picture of Father, conscious of her rank. She is
silly with me, but to others she is a Ramsdell, a teacher, the
daughter of Jacob. Her genuine affection for Luther
cannot hold itself back, though. She smiled and sparkled,
gracing his ball with sincere good will. The moon shone
brightly enough to read by, and as the company departed
and Luther and I hitched up Bruno to the wagon again,
Rosette scratched a few lines into her journal.

* * *

Once home again, Rosette and I took Bruno and the
wagon to the barn and then carried her things to the
house. People come and go around our farm, as some
come to confer about the land, and some buy our sugar.
Father is a Justice of the Peace—and he holds by force of
knowledge and strength his position in the community.
He is bringing me into that place, too. He invited me to go
for him to a Republican meeting at the white school house
this week. Last month he traveled to Kalamazoo to hear a
speech on behalf of Frémont for President—our only
hope for the nation, he says. Fillmore is all right, but in his
speech for Frémont Mr. Abraham Lincoln quipped that

Fillmore could be a man of the whole nation only because he wouldn't get votes from either side.[1] The Kalamazoo lawyer from whom Father bought our land invited Mr. Lincoln, another lawyer, to speak. And he wrote to invite Father, as well.

In this election it all comes down to the relation of one man to another. Three quarters of a century ago, when our people were in Massachusetts, the thing most pressing was to *get* a country, to beget it. Founders fell over themselves to agree even when they did not. The Crown set up in business on this shore, and if we were to take up our rightful ownership, we had still to take up what came with the land. Some colonies depended on slaves for their production, having inherited that way of life from their fathers. They came to the business innocently enough, by royal charter and inheritance. And some colonies had climates and geography unfriendly to slaved farms, or with other means of production.

Our grandfathers found distance from man-holding, and that made it all the more distasteful to our people. And perhaps they saw the advantages it gave the Southern planters and wanted to found the nation clean of it. But some knew the consonance of the colonies was too fragile, and could not withstand that question. So they put it off, for the sake of the Union.

Now, though, for the sake of the Union, for our purity and our moral health, and for the blessing of God—now we must cleanse ourselves. Father has helped me see this. And Frémont is our best hope to make the improvement, though we start small. We start by stopping slavery's spread.

---

[1]	http://www.kpl.gov/local-history/general/lincoln-speech.aspx

And so we spend our evenings at home—and our days with lighter work—discoursing with one another on these questions. Father takes me back to the principles of God, and I see their rightness. I am satisfied that we—and many in our state who agree—are setting this land on a sound course now. This will be my first election, and I am proud to cast my vote for Frémont.

* * *

In these last days Father has welcomed a new young fellow, my age, who wants to settle here, Otis Churchill. He is of our people back in New York and Massachusetts, so almost a cousin, I think, and nephew to Myron King. He is to help us burn, turning this forest into land for planting. He has a brisk and forceful way about him, always active with something, even if it is just a knife. He whittles as he visits with more idle folk by the stove of an evening.

Having arrived while Rosette was away at the Institute, Churchill stood at the door to welcome her, odd as that may be, when we walked up from the barn. He offered to take her maps, and she who had been most bold and forthright with Luther cast her eyes down and blushed as she handed them to him.

The next day McKelvey and Churchill came again and stayed all evening. Mr. Churchill asked Rosette if she would show him the neighborhood. He stood before her when he asked, feet planted on the front room carpet, and she looked up at him from her sewing chair, head down a little but eyes more bold. She set her sewing aside with one hand as she extended the other for him to take.

They walked to the Howes' and must have gone to Jerome and Frank's playhouse in the woods—I saw them come out from that direction after a few hours. We had years of fun ourselves in our playhouse back in

Kalamazoo, creating our own school and church and store as well as house. As soon as we could we made another here, used it almost reluctantly a year or two, knowing we had grown too old for it, and then ceded it to the youngsters. Ellen has now grown beyond it, too, but Rosette still goes there sometimes with her journal.

Again the next afternoon Otis, as we are calling him now, called for Rosette to show him the flats that Howe is burning at his place, in advance of our own work here. She tripped out quickly, leaving her sewing spread on a chair.

* * *

Now Otis is properly at work with Father, and Rosette at her own work. In fact, she has been called to Mrs. Bugbee's to sew there, across the river. Mother and Father do not seem to see the connection I see growing between Rosette and Otis. Perhaps they are just glad to see Otis a forward, ambitious fellow. The one Rosette fancied in Kalamazoo was content to sit about in parlors. We have a life to create here, out of the wilderness, not a town to sit about in while we talk of society scandals and topcoat fashions back East.

From the Journal of
Rosette Cordelia Ramsdell
October 1856

    Sunday 12th Otis came . . . with me . . . to the river & looked at that a while, which was almost covered with leaves. . . . I never saw such a day before. The world seemed to be completely filled with smoke, which hung dark & heavy, shrouding everything in that somber yellowish hue, but which was not altogether unpleasant.

Rosette - Fires

I AM GLAD THE BUGBEES live on a stage road, more traveled than ours, so that I can see glimpses of what is happening in the world beyond our wood while I stay here. The other day a number of teams passed, going to a political meeting in Portland. There were flags and even some four-horse teams and everyone in fine spirits. They didn't care whether we supported their man—Democrat or Republican. But they hoped, I think, to catch us up in their cause by their mere exuberance. And so they did. We are a patriotic folk in these lands—twenty years ago Berlin, I think it was, or Portland, with barely a clearing in the woods, held an Independence Day celebration. They had music and a log augured out to look like a cannon—called a "Quaker cannon." And in Jackson a while back was the first meeting of the Republicans, "under the oaks," they say.

I sat quiet in the Bugbees' front room with my hand work as they bustled about me preparing for their visiting excursion. They will take two wagons for all their folk and go past Grand Rapids to Grand Haven. Then on to the great sand hills, where the children have not yet been.

"It is a queer thing," I said at breakfast, "to be in the woods on this side and toil up through the sand. It is suddenly soft underfoot, where before was familiar firm ground."

"Is it sands as in Egypt, with a pyramid?" piped Henry. "I saw that in a book."

"No, but sudden," I said, looking to the interested faces about me and lowering my voice for effect. "As if the sands had started to grow out of the woods themselves. And when you struggle to the top you almost forget where you are going for concentrating on the effort. But as you come near the top you feel that something is about to happen. And suddenly the horizon comes into view—" Here I held my hands out to indicate the horizon. "Blue as far as you can see from left to right and almost forever in front of you. The clouds come to rest almost on the surface of the water, hovering in the distance."

"You tell that very well, Rosette," said Mrs. Bugbee, standing to begin clearing up. "I have seen it so myself. We are so closed in here, with the trees all about us. We cannot imagine what it is to see so far, until we've done so."

I thanked her, then added to Henry, "Be sure to have a little pail for building a sand castle down near the shore. You want a place where it is damp, as it is by the river in some places here. And you can build and dig moats. You'll want to bring down a branch from the other side for flags."

After breakfast I took my chair over by the door to finish a shirt for Mr. Bugbee to have fresh for visiting. My needle flies swift and sure, drawing a garment together as it dives and emerges like some water insect dancing along the river. It is odd to be part of a household, yet not part of it. I am able to have my own leisure of sorts while they have all the worry—and excitement—of their preparations. The people come and go even more here than at our place. It is natural for the easy road before them here. Cousin Thomas Ramsdell was one of these last night. I hadn't seen this youngest of Uncle Ganet's in years, and glad I was to be here for the treat. He is trim, smart, noble, and handsome, and just such a one as should make a hero for a novel. He brought his little trick dog Bony, and made him to ask me a blessing.

The little round-bellied thing staggered across the floor to me, its tiny white paws folded down before its shoulders, its eyes great rounds of brown appealing for my favor. I laughed as I was meant to and took up the little beggar in my lap. His cool, wet nose snuffled against my hand as he wriggled and licked with pleasure, his performance complete.

"Cousin Rosette," Thomas asked, very familiar but gallant, still. "Might you come to us for the winter? You could keep Mother company now that Leonora has her own home. You ought not be shut up in the wood."

"But my own mother needs me for all the work on our place," I answered. "I do the hand-work while she tends the table, in the main. And we are not so much shut up anymore, as the folks are burning even now and making the road." I thought of Otis swinging his axe against the trunks and wiping his brow with his arm. Solomon and the boys and Father do their part, too, with the neighbors. A little at a time, with great labor, they clear the land.

With a sharp whistle Thomas summoned Bony, who scrambled out of my lap and across the floor to him. Standing Bony up on his lap, working his forelegs like a puppet's arms, Thomas made as if to speak for the little dog, in a high voice: "Well, we would be obliged if you would come, in any case." I smiled and took up my work again.

Cousin Thomas appeals to me, I thought, as the stitches formed a line down the placket. I would add my mark, a tiny embroidered maple leaf, above the second button-hole, once that line was done. Then I would finish the left cuff. But of course he is too near a cousin, so we may banter and play and mean nothing by it, as if to practice for real wooing. I can play like that with Luther, as well. It is understood that we have no common future.

But Otis is a promising suitor and his interest seems in earnest. When he holds out a hand to me and I take it, he translates strength through his grip, drawing me wherever it is he will go. He comes of good people, so that is all right, and has plans that match his efforts—Daddy seems to approve him.

When I finished the cuff of the blue checked shirt I shook it out to straighten, then folded it neatly for Mrs. Bugbee to pack—no sense ironing what will soon be rumpled in a bag. I took my leave of the Bugbees and Cousin Thomas and set off home again, calling at one farm along the way for dinner and to collect my two dollars school money. I used a part of that for eight pounds lard of Mr. King, as Mother had asked. As I approached home I could see they were shutting up the house, off to a Republican meeting at the school house. Mother gave each of us a hunk of bread with ham tucked into it, and carried a jug of cider to pass around, and I climbed into the wagon and joined them.

Our new-built school house is a neat little thing, with its title, "Orange School House District No. 1 1845," over the front window rim. Father was the teacher then, with Sol and I as pupils. Diana attended when she was well enough, and a few others. This new school house has a clever design, and visitors are glad to see it.

When a teacher stands at the teacher's desk with all eyes upon him—or her—he has all the pupils before him and to either side, arranged in ranks, each row a little higher than the one in front of it. Mr. Badger, who helped build the Capitol in Lansing, built this place to be like a theatre in ancient times. The more learned teachers make the most of that setting, reminding scholars of the noble Greeks and Romans. Or they recite from *Hamlet* or some such. Solomon, in one of the night schools last year, brought goose flesh upon me with his Patrick Henry— "Give me liberty or give me death!"

But even in our old school building—quite a plain one—I often dreamed of being a teacher myself. A Ramsdell almost cannot help being a teacher, I think. My talents turn more to the sums and memorization than to the declamation and logic of the advanced pupils. It's needed, my teaching, and I expect to do the winter term again here, unless . . .

It felt patriotic of us all to gather there at the school house, but it seemed the expected speakers from Ionia were not coming, so Mr. Brown and Father addressed us all. When Father stood at the meeting to speak, I was glad to be his daughter and sat still and listened. He spoke his own words and those of that lawyer, Mr. Abraham Lincoln, he'd heard last month. And he made a little fun, too. Mr. Lincoln said of his rival on the podium, "Douglas is a great man—at keeping from answering questions he don't want to answer."[2] They all liked that, guffawing and clapping.

But then Father got sober. He told us that Mr. Lincoln had charged that slavery was not only the greatest question, but nearly the only question. My heart swelled and I thought it impossible anyone could think of voting for Buchanan. Ours is the noble cause—to keep slavery from the new lands. The men agreed, and the gathering elected both Father and Mr. Brown as delegates to the county convention.

---

[2] http://www.kpl.gov/local-history/general/lincoln-speech.aspx

As we arrived home, I paused by the lantern Mother hung at the door as she went in. I felt for the clasp on my pinned watch and popped it open to see that it was half past eleven. A long day.

Next day all was as usual with comings and goings and my own visits, including to Elder Lee's in the afternoon for Amos Utter to be married to Nancy Allen. It was beautiful in the sunshine, the just-turning leaves rustling in the breeze. We all gathered in the yard while the couple stood before Elder Lee on the front steps. The goldenrod bent against Nancy's skirts, and the wind blew her pink bonnet ribbons out against Amos's strong arm, as if to embrace him. He's made a good choice in an excellent girl, and I know she'd had her eye on him for a while, quietly waiting for him to notice her, but ready to answer his interest with her own. I watched them and wondered when it might be my turn. Did they really think about those words in the vows? Does one have to mean it at the time for the vow to hold? Or does it just rush past in the excitement?

But in another hour we had eaten a bite of cake and said our congratulations and were home again as if nothing more momentous had occurred than the purchase of a new calf. Father received a caller bringing a span of horses and wagon and fifty dollars for forty acres. Father shows what increase may be made here.

I see details like these in my journal and know they tell my days, but cannot tell what really consumes all my thoughts—Otis. He first came to us while I was away at Lyons. When I first laid eyes on him he was at our door, as if he were the householder. He is powerful and quick, middling in stature but not in dynamism (that word from one of my novels, surely)—he seems much larger than he is. And the room fairly crackles with him in it, glowing red-hot as within a smoldering log. But will it all crumble away into nothingness and ashes at a touch? I can feel him behind me in the yard, or pick out his voice in an instant. Yet he seems not to take note of me except at times entirely at his design.

He startled me at supper that night when he was in deep conference with Daddy and Sol and Amos Utter, who came to work with them. They were laying out the plan for cutting trees and burning stumps from the land the next day. It must be carefully done to contain the fire, and to make the most of the men available to work. They arranged the cups and knives on the table as our place, and the road, and so forth. All that business that seemed not to have anything to do with Mother and me and the children. But Otis lifted his brown head from among the fair and peppered and coal-black to acknowledge my presence. As if he were saying, "Yes, I see you there, and will attend to you presently."

Fair Solomon is cool water to Otis's heat. My brother recalls the smooth swells of the river, gliding constant, all of one substance, rolling and shining, from one sure source along the way to harbor, opening then to all the world. All is his home, and he at ease within it. Otis flickers and leaps, sparks and singes. But it is all contained in the armor of a stove, fixed and solid—cool, even, when the fire is not kindled.

But Otis was not so cool when we were alone at the boys' playhouse last week. He was all in a rush about homesteads and sugar and how Father could give him the advantage he needed. It was easy for me then to see him busy in his thoughts as men are, and talking to me without all that men's dignity. It is pomposity, really, when they are in a gathering with women. Or even just among themselves, they boast to cut a figure.

Right away, that first day when we took a walk in the woods, he looked at me frankly and said, "And with your reputation for the needle, and proven strong mind . . .

Well, you've kept a school for years! You would be just the one, and your father's daughter, too."

"Well," I answered, pretending not to notice that "just the one" in his speech, "I suppose I have been brought up with all this business. I even have my own little commerce in the schools. It is rather my own way of farming—planting the figures and poems in little heads, then waiting months to go about gathering my harvest in school fees."

"And do you know all the other house-ways—baskets and soap and baking and all?" He had set one foot on the window sill of the playhouse as if he meant to stride clear over the top of it. He could have done it, with all the energy that kept him shifting and leaning as he spoke, breaking twigs across his knee.

"Of course," I said, "Though I hardly notice the work of the kitchen, being caught up in sewing and knitting for us and others." I stood straight and quiet by a little sapling a few feet away.

"I've heard of your reputation in that, from Mr. Ramsdell."

Why would Father offer such comment to a new sojourning laborer at our place? Mother and I were usually the engine of the house, essential to its running and dear to him in private, but not to be discussed freely with others in that way.

"Indeed?"

"Well, I asked him right out, to know what is his situation in all respects," Otis answered. "Your father is a man well known for his prosperity and sound business dealings. I mean to learn of him."

"And he is glad for willing pupils," I said. "I may have kept a school here and there, but he is more a teacher than I am."

Otis Churchill is so different from Timothy. That one is no doubt, as I think on it, on a sateen cushion in a house somewhere in Kalamazoo. That is how he was when I kept school there. He bantered with ladies and had no other aim for his future than to continue that way. I could never get from him how he expected to make his way in the world. He smiled and flattered me, showing my miniature around. But I couldn't see past a sunny afternoon with him. He spoke like some of those witty fellows in novels—I have learned they are in real life not worth so much as the paper used to write about them. When I came home from there I was determined to make my own way, to do things as I see fit. In my dress, for instance . . .

In Kalamazoo a young lady would from time to time wear the bloomer dress to call up conversation, and she would flaunt the silken drawers in Turkish style, with light slippers, as in the magazines they passed around. But I soon saw the use of such an arrangement for farm work. When I came home to Mother and Father I began with one of my older dresses, cutting off fourteen inches of its length, and shortening a petticoat to match. I fashioned summer trousers that reached to my ankles, secured with ribbon ties, and enjoyed such practical improvement I could not see why everyone did not wear her skirts thus. The skirts last longer, not being dragged into manure nor caught upon brambles, not tripping a woman up as she makes her way through the house and up and down stairs. I have much freedom from the sheer weight of all that fabric cut away. And in winter my flannel bloomers are quite cozy and not as liable to catch alight as are Mother's great skirts. But the ladies of Lyons and Ionia shift their eyes sidelong at me when I am in town, and though my neighbors and family have grown used to me, they have not yet joined me.

Otis does not seem to mind my singular fashion. To him I seem already to be a part of a grand plan for an important future, short skirts or no. It is good to see one work with such fervor at everything he puts his hand to. Alacrity and intensity—that's what he has. I am in one hour sure he is sweeping me up in his plans from the outset, having been struck with my suitability for him. But in another moment I think he looks right through me to the next thing on a list. He keeps one in a little book always in his pocket, with a small knife-sharpened pencil.

Pencil and ink, I suppose we would be if we were man and wife. He is quick and hard-driven, always moving on to the next thing, not caring whether the smudged gray will last past the next chore. But I take care with my journal and my ink and pen. I make little stitches of the letters laid down in my book, binding up the days in remembrance as if smocking a baby's dress in fine detail. And what is the substance of what I tuck in there? Names and the temperature and wind of the day. How many pounds of beef or sugar that Daddy has or inches of stocking I've worked on that day, on that particular ticking by of time, as my own watch ticks tiny, pinned above my heart.

What is a heart, anyway, but a silly woman's notion, or a girl's, drawn up from books instead of real life? I see little heart in Mama—she is all grim bustle most times. She let out a sad little sigh when she first saw my bloomer dress but knew it was no good to mention it. She asks me sharp questions and tips her head and narrows her eyes to listen for what she fears. She distrusts what I say, or discounts it. The older I grow, still unwed, the worse it gets. But she surprises me sometimes—her hand trembles a moment when we come across some little thing of poor Diana's in the house. Then she softens and looks far into the distance. Daddy has a big heart, like an enchanted jolly bear in a story, but he is chained when beyond our private table.

Can the love in books come true for us? Or is it like a fairies' ball, magical and sparkling but made for a girl of ten or twelve, to dissolve away to mushrooms at dawn? I am a girl of twenty-six who should properly be a woman by now. I have my miniature back from Timothy, and I wonder, shall I entrust it to Otis? As I look around, I see younger girls securing their futures with husbands and having the first earnest in a year's crop of a single infant, or two. My suitors have not yet suited, I suppose.

* * *

The burning increases day to day. At first it sent hazy wisps of smoke drifting over from the Howes' the day I showed Otis, and now we are not able to see six rods before us. In fact Otis, who was chopping at Mr. Howe's for two days, came to fetch Sol to help. But they had to give it up. *I never saw the like. O dear the smoke is so near the ground & so thick that we can see but about a rod distinctly.*

I wrote of that today just before the ink spilled. It blotted my book a bit, but mostly streamed across the table and into my lap. More washing. Our washing will be saffroned with smoke, no doubt, to remind us in days to come of what these days were like.

We made a dancing party, though, in the midst of the yellow billows, Sol playing for us. We were twenty couples, single and married and babes and all—Luther, Amos and Nancy the newlyweds, and a dozen others. And of course Otis was with us. He was surprisingly apt at the dance, which I would not have expected for all his seriousness about business. Solomon stamped twice and flourished his fiddle to call us to attention, then scraped a bit comically, drawing out whoops and laughter. Then he lilted the first notes of "Gal on a Log," and we fell into our places. The men lined straight as soldiers facing the "pretty maids in a row," as Sol called us, we all expectant and rosy and smiling. Otis seemed stiff and grim in his face, but he made the steps his business and me his partner. With the yellow haze even in the house it was a kind of magical fairy-ball for us.

It didn't dissolve away into sweet sleep as it does for the fairies, though, and I lay abed for hours, my eyes wide in the dark, thinking of much.

Next night Otis took me on a moonlit walk far past midnight. Despite two nights of staying up too late, I had to continue my work, though I could hardly keep my eyes open.

I trust my dreams to carry along in sleep what I have not time for in my busy days. But I do not know what my dreams mean, if anything. I wrote about one of them: *I dreamed of going over a mountain, at the foot of which lay a large river. As I passed over, a tumbling torrent kept pouring along at my left, which looked at once terrific, grand, and enchanting.* When have I seen mountains recently, but for being reminded of the sand hills the Bugbees are visiting now? I saw some long ago in New York and Pennsylvania, but have not been there since I was a babe. Would Mother say that Otis is a mountain, or does the dream signify him as the torrent? Or must I get beyond my many fears and get on with life? It seems to be forming itself in a path before me—I would that I could see the way!

From the Journal of
Rosette Cordelia Ramsdell
November 1856

Tuesday 18th. Otis cut his foot, but he would go to Mr. Kings & after getting there his foot was so bad he had to stay. I hope he will keep still a little while, so as not to be laid up all winter, but he is so ambitious it will be hard work for him.

Wednesday 19th. Frank's 5th birth day. . . . Otis came just before supper. Warm & pleasant. Dreamed I went to Lyons, & to see Mrs. Mortimer, to ask her about the price of dresses & bonnets as I wished to get some. She asked me if I knew a family, living near where I did, by the [name] of Ramsdell. She had heard of Rosette Ramsdell a great deal & would like very much to see her. I told her yes, but didn't tell her I was the one.

Sally - Dreams

OH, SO BUSY HERE, the work not caring we have an election! Extra dishes for all the visitors and the men at their chopping—hungry work it is. And the washing as lief as not done, for all the smoke from their burning for our road and fields. But then none can see right clearly, in any case, so the ash settled in the front room makes no matter. I'd not have it in the butter, though. I keep Rosette and Ellen on tip-toe to keep it all in order.

With Jacob a delegate—and John Brown—we are part of the pageant for the Presidential campaign. I am a proud wife, hoping to do Jacob Ramsdell honor, and I can do a bit of that with the housekeeping.

When our men went to Ionia last month to the Republican mass meeting, I went along and marveled at the three thousand in attendance! We all had badges—ten inches of red satin and white watered ribbon, headed by an eagle. The names of Frémont and Dayton, and below that a portrait of Frémont—so handsome. Then words that make me proud—"Free speech and free men—Slavery shall not travel into Kansas by our votes." One of our districts in this area is nine tenths for abolition. I was proud of the thirty-two women from Lyons who went, portraying the states, with "Kansas" in a black cape. No time for a farm wife to do that politicking, but—oh!—I am so glad to have seen it!

In all Jacob's campaign business and the new school district for the new pupils coming in with their families, I am sometimes here alone to keep the house. I did have a fright that day a wagon came up, with two grown men, a young one, and two women who wanted to stop here. I feared what Jacob would say—no matter who they were themselves. So I said, politely, "I am afraid we cannot keep you very well here." I hoped they would just drive on. Oh, but they were tired, and had come out of their way. Could they just sleep on the floor or any old place? I was beginning to feel fretful as they pressed. The young man threw one leg out of the back of the wagon to come down, and I wrung the dish-cloth I had carried from the kitchen. Where WAS Rosette just then?

At last, one said, "I suppose you don't know us, then?"

"Well, no—do I know you?!" And suddenly, as if that yellow haze had cleared, I saw that it was Polly, and I rushed out to the gate. "Cousin Noah, I declare, you old scamp, how do you do?!" They introduced me to young Daniel Watson, the one who frightened me by starting to climb out of the wagon. Rosette came outside by then and we had a time, laughing and shouting and pushing about. Later when Jacob arrived, he himself did not know them, and we had some more of the same fun. When they left the next day, I realized I could not account for Rosette, nor Otis, for some of the time of the visit.

In the pleasant autumn we are having now they disappear for hours at a time, off in the woods somewhere or along the road. And they need an eye upon them—she is not so aloof as she ought to be. She was sure about not wanting that Timothy in Kalamazoo—and rightly so, Jacob said, though she mooned and moaned about him long afterward.

But then suddenly, as naturally as sunshine follows rain, it seems she has forgotten all that. She has made her choice in Otis Churchill, giving him her miniature. She's nearly twenty-seven, so I am relieved. I don't really know his people, beyond his being a nephew of Mrs. King, and that he was a farm laborer in my old Ontario County in New York. He works with a fierceness to him, and because he does not take much notice of me, I may watch him without care. I determined he would do and told Jacob so. I fear Jacob is becoming as anxious as I to see Rosette wed, and has forgotten some of his lofty old standards.

* * *

The betrothal is made, and now that Rosette will be a new wife instead of teacher, we must bring on a new schoolteacher to take her place in the winter term—Daniel Watson's sister may be a good prospect.

And the sooner the wedding the better. That Otis prowls the house like a panther. I'm always glad to see him go out to his work, though it may be the end of him yet. Endlessly chopping, he cut his wrist terribly and was to rest a few days but was out again in one—again chopping. Rosette hangs on his words, making herself as ridiculous as a girl of sixteen. She will not talk to me of her affections but shares her dreams as if they did not signify, curiosities like whatever might pass by on the road in a day. She dreams of riding horseback, and of stage actresses leading her with candles deep into unknown stairwells. She dreams of Jacob setting house fires to ward off robbers—I don't need Cousin Betsy Packard's cards and candles to know what churns in her heart.

We must come and go, and I am always wary of how long they might be here alone without some folks of the family to guard—without seeming to. Or, as with the little boys, without knowing they do. Between Providence and me, we can keep them to the New Year, can we not? And then all will be well.

After our Thanksgiving, when Otis was back chopping "against all remonstrance," as Rosette says, she considered her stores. She does not have much for a household. To begin at the beginning, with herself, she went to Lyons for plain white muslin and deep red—she says "maroon"—flowered paramatta.[3] Fifty cents a yard—good it is that she has a tiny figure and not my matronly one. And she does have an advantage in economy with her short skirts—less fabric is needed. I did long to think of her in a long dress for her wedding, though.

"Rosette," I told her, "I would be pleased to use my little store of savings to buy you blue silk for your dress for the wedding, if you will make it a long one."

"Would you, Mother?" she smiled, biting the thread from a button she was sewing onto a shirt. "I don't think I should like it long, as I have grown so used to the short."

"But it would look so well on you. And for such an occasion—and other important ones later, when you are a married woman."

"I do not think it would be honest of me to wear something for my wedding that I never wear at any other time. No, Otis chose me in short skirts, and he will have me thus."

And thus it will be—the short red dress, bloomers to match. She ordered a hat, as well—three dollars. She will look fine with her clear blue eyes and dark blonde hair swept over her ears. Her hands are in a state, not like the hands of a bride in a book. But Dr. Killey will make her

---

[3] a lightweight wool blend fabric

some salve for the salt rheum.[4] I can see that she keeps her hands out of too much water, I doing that kind of work for now, but she will be in a fix when she has her own house— or shanty to start. There all is harder, closed in with the low roof and but one window.

Here the young ones make their start that way, while we got used to married life with a proper house back in New York. I am glad they will do it with our house just up the road to help. Now it is wholly ours, since Jacob made it pay for itself two years ago. So many more settle here now than when we first came to this land to work it a decade ago. But back then all was quiet wood, and the river. We had no more than wagon and walking paths here, and not even that through most of our land. A few frame buildings made a town. Those who feared wolves and bears and Indians, as I did, dug in right near the town and now find themselves in the midst of it. But after wearying of the bustle in Kalamazoo, Jacob would press out what seemed then so far. He secured what looked to be half the county. What would we ever do with it? Now, as we make our own little farm-town where we are out here, others come to buy sugar of us, and land nearby, the road beginning to go in. How it has changed!

My house is to be the workshop as the men make a cutter for us. Fine it will be for the young couple to take on their wedding journey, flying along through the snow along the river. Meantime I lose my front room and the best south light for close work. No matter who comes to the house, the men and boys go to the workbench there. I must keep the door shut against all the sawdust and scrap. Yesterday Ellen, not sure whether she's girl or woman, poked her head into the kitchen, finger to her lips, and motioned that I follow. We went on tip-toes to the front

---

[4] a form of eczema

room and there I saw the little boys with the plane, scraping away. They scattered when I put my head in the room, but no harm done.

Nephew Charles—with us for the month—is a likely boy and sticks close to Solomon. "Sol and Charley" can always be found together—at the chopping, butchering the hog, off in the wagon to town. The little fellow is great with trap and gun and brought us a mink the other day, and three quail another. Just thirteen, he picked his farm and then changed his mind and made a good trade for a better one. How can he be both man and the most boy-like boy I've ever known? I like seeing him play sometimes with the little boys. Jerome, at eight, has a sense of his own dignity, but little Frank follows Charley like a puppy. I'm glad to have him in the house—it eases the loss of Diana a little. Just this little handful of years she has been gone . . .

When Rosette and Otis have their own place, by summer, perhaps we can board the schoolteachers a bit more than we do now, and find Sol a bride that way! I needn't worry, though. At all the parties, he with his fiddle and trimmed flaxen beard, the young ladies are watching him, and he them. He has his father's deep thoughts. He will want a wife more fine than I—more like Rosette, but deeper still. Rosette is all order and form, but Solomon calls out deep and quavery on his fiddle for some bride who can answer that call.

* * *

One day last week Sol shed himself of Charley for a bit and took Rosette to Lyons, where they found all in an uproar. Four stores opposite the hotel burned up in the night, and Rosette said the remains still glowed and smoked. Now Fox and the others must start again, but were insured for one thousand dollars each. That could make a pretty fine new store, maybe with some of that stained glass across the tops of bow windows.

We use the fire here to do our work, but we know it can destroy as well. Just last month that fire below us took sixteen tons of hay. It is a mercy no one was killed.

So no hat for Rosette, but she got her salve, and an invitation to another party. I cannot wait to see how she overmakes the hat she has to cut a figure at the party. Ellen watches and longs herself to be invited. Her day will come soon enough.

On Sunday, with a few inches of snow, the horse got the colic and broke the wagon while we were at meeting. But Sol and Otis fixed it quick so Solomon could venture out this pleasant day to fetch Miss Mary White, our new teacher, who will make her home here to start. She will be a third in the bed with the girls, or Ellen on a pallet on the floor. As Ellen got her settled up there, Rosette set the table early for supper.

"Oh, Mama!" Rosette cried, holding the forks to her breast like an actress. "When she came with her satchel on her arm I thought it was me! I don't know how I will manage without the school myself. It seems so strange not to teach this term."

"Well, you are moving on to other things, and cannot have the school, too." I cast pepper into the sausage—I would not have her hurt her hands in that. She settled down on a bench to darn and talk to me while Ellen came down from where Mary was upstairs unpacking. Ellen looked to what needed doing and went out to take the wash off the line. Charley and Jerome made themselves useful, bringing in wood, while Frank stayed underfoot.

"I had a dream about that, you know," Rosette said, amidst all the bustle. "About the school."

"—And put it in your journal, no doubt," I answered.

"Indeed, with the others. If I do not write the dreams right away, I lose them. In this one I had taken a school.

The first day arrived, and I opened the door to find young men and women, not little ones. I asked them, as usual, what readers they used, and there were hardly two of them alike in the whole school!"

"That would be a fix, I'm sure."

"They commenced reading, and one girl of thirteen or fourteen was making trouble. I took her aside, but it did no good—she was just as bad two minutes later. I found all the scholars to be pretty fractious generally."

"And was that all?" I asked.

"At the end I left and went to Mr. Smith's farm."

"Why there? They have nothing to do with schools usually, for all Luther was a good student."

"Well, Mother, I cannot explain my dreams—I just tell you what happens in them! So I sat down with Mr. Smith, and I must have looked frightened, by what I could see in his face looking at me, and I told him of my ill luck."

"And then?" Anyone would be foolish to confide in Frog Smith, or frightened if she must.

"Well, that was all. But a better dream followed. At Cousin Noah's, a very large house, by the way—"

"—Oh, he would like that, and she, too!" I exclaimed, holding up my hand for her to pause. The boys had just come in with another load of wood. "Frank, Jerome— would you go see to the cow? It's milking time." I motioned to Rosette to continue.

"—At their house, John had improved a great deal in fiddling." We both laughed to remember his screeching with Sol that day a couple of years ago. "As John was playing one day," she went on, "Cousin Polly came into the room to play on an instrument like a big guitar, only round, with a bow to draw across the center, covered with leather."

"How would that work?" I asked.

"I don't know—it was a dream!—but it was covered with small slits, and she asked me to play, and I did very well to make an excellent bass or second to John."

"Well, that is good," I said. "You attain much in your dreams!" Just then the boys came tumbling back into the room for the pail they'd forgotten, and that was the end of it. Tomorrow they'll be at the school and things will be calmer here.

*From the Journal of
Rosette Cordelia Ramsdell
December 1856*

Wednesday 3rd. Charles went to Lyons, & brought me a pamphlet, a sample of a new kind of first & second reader, sent I suppose by some of the Professors, & which was addressed to R. C. Ramsdell Esq.

Tuesday 9th. We all spent the evening at Mr. Howe's, with the exception of Father & Charles, & we had a nice time. We girls went out . . . to the big hill coasting, & the boys were there too. We were afraid to ride down alone so the boys drawed us.

Sunday 14th. Four inches of snow fell during the night & continued falling all day. Otis went to Mr. Kings to be gone a week or two, & I am lonely.

Rosette - Preparations

I JUST CANNOT GET THE SCHOOL out of my thoughts, with Mary White here again this week, and the new readers sent to me as if I were still a teacher: "R.C. Ramsdell Esq." Didn't Jerome have fun with that, dancing around the house to mock me with the letter? I seem so heated with all manner of things that my dreams are frightening me now. I dare not tell Mother of this last, which makes me ridiculous, but I'll put it in my journal. I dreamed I was teaching, and some of the large girls wore quite a beard, and shaved. The younger wanted to do the same, but the older were jealous and did not want to give up their advantage, so they quarreled.

Next day I visited Miss White's school and bypassed our place on the way back to go on to Mr. Howe's, where most of our folks joined me for a coasting party. We had antics like children, tumbling off the sleds and throwing snow-balls from behind the trees. Thrice I was able to go down the long hill by myself, thundering through the stinging spray as the afternoon sun sank behind the hill.

All became blue and gray around me and grew quiet as I trudged back up, the last to go inside.

I found there the folks all talking of the election results. So Frémont will not be our man, but Buchanan. It does not seem auspicious to have our menfolk voting for the losing party, as if that made us somehow foolish. But I cannot truly concern myself with it. For Mother it is an enthusiasm, and for Father and Solomon a dire business. I do not think I have heard Otis say a word for one candidate or another, so it is no use my having a concern for it.

Some days I feel a child and see children around me being grown folks, like Ellen, with her quiet watchfulness. Charles helped for a few days to get our new cutter ironed, with trips back and forth to Ionia and Portland. Then, in his little manly way, he took our old cutter and his old horse and went home to Montcalm. I will miss him, and Ellen will lose the banter she had with him as he played the part of a suitor. Jerome and Sol will sorely feel the loss of his work and company, but little Frank, too. He worshipped "Cholly," and I expect we'll hear of "Cholly" for many days to come.

With his leaving, and then Otis going to his uncle, Mr. King, and on a short journey, the house is quiet as the snows sift down on us each night and day. Here I am, shiftless even with a mountain of work to complete. That alpaca wool is a pleasure to cut and stitch, though, and I love to think of how it will suit me, and lie smooth over my new petticoat and hoops. And the paramatta—deep maroon and elegant even in the short length. What will Otis think when I wear it on our wedding trip? I am eager to be actually married, to have our union full and proper and get on with life.

Between us, Otis and I have a secret understanding that we are already really husband and wife, before God as Adam and Eve were. But we are burdened with the waiting and propriety. When we have a few moments alone he reaches out a hand to touch my face in compelling power, to remind me of the times we have more privacy to be who we really are to one another. I keep urging the days to pass quickly, that the calendar time, clock time, can catch up with us. It is only weeks until the world knows us as man and wife.

When he first spoke to me it was as if he already possessed me and waited only the chosen day to make it so. Power is the word that best describes him, and not power like Father's. No, Father is the grand man of the house, with his voice to hold all together, persuading and commanding as suits those he speaks with. I remember feeling so proud of Otis in his early days with us, when two other young men came to us for work. Father was courteous but distant, holding off as if he could tell something was amiss. He spoke with them, took them up to the barn about some work or other, and sent Jerome scurrying down to the house to tell Mother they'd be joining us for dinner.

Meanwhile, Otis was about some task, intent upon it, not worrying about these others who might take his place. I watched from the window. He stood by the little tree on the rise, in conference with the horses watering there, helping one that almost lost a shoe in the muck.

The two visitors were not quite right, I could tell when they came in. The tall, thin one did not even bother to wash his hands before the meal. Father has trained us to see things as he sees them, and he defers to Mother's judgment in much.

At dinner Father was very formal and scarcely spoke to Mother. The two men took that signal to ignore her altogether, as if she were a servant, and they fell to their food without a thought for decorum. They did not seem particularly famished—that would have been forgivable. But they scattered crumbs, and one crumpled his cap right on the tablecloth. I saw looks pass between Mother and Father, and Otis once caught my eye. The men answered too eagerly and without the firmness of men well used to work. They made promises without pith, is how I have heard Daddy say it. When we finished, Father stood and extended his arm to the door, with perfect courtesy, inviting the men to the front room and thence to the door. The round one tousled Frank's head roughly, but in a friendly way, as he stepped out. We knew we'd not see them again, that Father wouldn't want them.

But Otis shone, knowing just what Father wanted, because he wants those things himself, or most of them. Where Father is a man of words and still silence, meetings and speeches and school doings, Otis is a man of action. He does not long for books as I do, but he reads well and is willing to read aloud when asked. It just doesn't seem to kindle his spirit as it does mine. When he sees a thing he wants, he lights out for it, no matter the pain to get it.

He has chosen his place among the available holdings, just to the west on our road, and what a beautiful sugar-bush it has! He has not done maple sugar before but is determined to learn our ways with that and sugar off this next year. He is collecting his taps and pails in a corner of our barn until he has his own. As he builds and furnishes his shanty he will bring me there, and we will have a home of our own. We've talked of it on our walks, and out at the playhouse, bending our backs to duck inside like children. Then smiles become kisses and earnest grasping as flames kindle between us. Oh, to have a home of our own, to possess!

* * *

While Otis is away I feel I am almost holding my breath, doing things in a daze as I hurry to finish before the day of our marriage. But it will come no matter what, and the work can be done later—it will still be there. As long as I have my trousseau done, that will be enough. It is not far to the Kings', but the snow and our work hold us apart just now.

Life goes on here . . . and death. Mrs. Mousehunt has been failing for weeks and months, and we have sat vigil at her bedside, doing for the family as we can, in turns. One day I take my first sleigh ride of the winter, and another I meet a girl sewing a ball dress. I finally have my hat, and someone has a babe. It all goes 'round and whirls my thoughts, with no time to stop and feel just one thing.

When I returned from that trip to town I found I had been sent for. Poor Mrs. Mousehunt had died. Mrs. Kinney took little Martha home to care for her, and Mother and I stayed.

Mother and Mrs. Kinney bathed and dressed Mrs. Mousehunt's body, and she lay—or the body lay—in the bed with a ruffled nightcap and a coverlet pulled up to the chin. Mother went into the kitchen on some task, and I was alone, yet not alone. Mrs. Mousehunt's face was smooth and waxy in death, finally resting after fighting the fever with deep wrinklings of her brow. I knew her spirit was not there, but every creak of the house made me start, as if her spirit flew around in search of some place to light.

Was she at rest, really? Did she know someone would care for orphaned Martha, the rest already grown? When Diana died . . . was she at rest, knowing Father and all of us would care for Mother, the one who would mourn her most?

What of me? What if I were to take ill suddenly, or fall into the river and be bundled beneath the surface in a twist of skirts and a dragging of my heavy shoes? Would Otis mourn me as his wife? Or would he soon find another likely girl—younger—and make his farm with her?

I shivered at the thought and went on shivering. No one had brought in wood enough, and a storm blew about. We stayed vigil in the bedroom all night, I never having suffered so much with cold in my life. I kept on my cloak and curled up in my chair with a quilt. I tucked my hands in my arm-pits, my scarf around my head and across my mouth. And still I felt the numbness creep up my fingers and toes, and make my teeth ache as I drew breath. I thought I should freeze and was not ever warm while I stayed there.

Next day of course we must do the shroud, so Mother cut it before going home to make breakfast, and I sewed a little on it, tempted to baste rather than make the lovely seams folk praise me for. For what wear or show would this garment have? But I took care in any case, hoping it was seen in secret. I left for home before dinner, dreaming of our glowing stove, and met a cheerful sight—Charles had come back, and a little later Otis, much sooner than even he had thought!

So all attended the funeral next day, with a sermon by Elder Gown. Then, to make things as mixed up as ever they were, with life and death and happy and sad, I went home to Mr. King's with Otis and they pressed me to stay all night. The cold moderated to a rainstorm that blew and slashed and kept me watching. I will not say what else happened there, but "sunshine and shadows" could well describe the time, and next day we went home.

On the twenty-third dear Charley went to Ionia and brought home nuts and candy that he put in the children's stockings to make a Christmas for them. He gave Ellen a silk tulip on a pin and made her blush. I think sometimes these little gifts account more to the joy of the one who treats than to the one who receives the gift, for Charley was as all-over dimples as little Frank. Jerome couldn't help his own delight as he ran out for the nut cracker and showed Frank how to turn the screw to crack the shells.

Otis was invited to a party in Ionia and we made it otherwise a work day. Mary White and the girls came here after school and asked me to go home with them to supper, it being both Christmas and Elsie's birthday. They would not take no for an answer. And though our talk kept turning back to Otis and my dresses and hats and plans, he was not really the substance of my thoughts. I was as caught up in chatter as they, so I did not miss Otis so much. I should have been doing work instead, for I have much to do!

These days alternate snowy, sunny, and rainy. One morning the ground and everything was covered with ice and the fences fringed with icicles. Only Sol went to meeting that day at the white school house. If I had done it, it would have seemed a show, but Solomon is all sincerity.

The day is coming very soon. Each morning carries me closer to my marriage. Last night I dreamed I packed my things and got ready to start for Kalamazoo—to teach, I suppose—and a man came to hire me to teach in this district. Well, that's almost what is happening to me—a man is calling me to stay in this district, though I do not think he wants teaching! I am not the only one preparing, though. Father had a tooth out that was bothering him, so that it would not interrupt our party. And Mr. Brower sent twelve dollars for Otis, to be expended by chopping on his farm—Otis's first work as a husband, when we return. What a nice wedding present!

1857 MICHIGAN

From the Journal of
Rosette Churchill
January 1857

    1st. Another new year. And the day was a beautiful one, & one that will be remembered by me as being the happiest in my life; as I was joined in the holy & happy bonds of marriage with the man, whom above all the earth I sincerely love & respect. That man is Otis Churchill. . . . O the clouds have all passed from the sky of my life & I bathe in a flood of sunshine. And I hope it will be so ever, & I feel confident that it will. I shall try; always try so to act, as to render the days of him who has chosen me as a partner on the earth: calm & peaceful. The fathomless depths of feeling are stirred from their remotest recesses when I consider my position as relating to this, the purest & strongest tie of mortals. Now if I fulfill, faithfully the part assigned me, my life, which I have deplored so often will not have been in vain.

Otis - Journey

I T IS DONE. I have a likely wife, whose father has aided my plans and who draws me closer to him to good advantage. I am well into the family now, and shall be.

A crowd came a few at a time for the rite—King and his brood, the McKelveys and neighbor Howes with their girls, and the Elder Gown and wife. I knew all these, but some cousins of Rosette's were there, and another fellow—Luther, they called him—sidled in before sunset. He said it was the first time he'd ever seen two pairs of pants married. Rosette just kissed his cheek friendly-like and introduced us—told me they'd grown up together. Sol and the new teacher stood up with us for the vows, and the missus—now Mother Ramsdell to me—served cake.

"For your birthday, too, Otis, not just the wedding!" she said.

Sol's music, dancing, all as usual. I was for hours ready to be on our way, but it was after midnight when we set off to Uncle Myron's. All wished us good luck as we bundled into their cutter, from one crowd to another. Uncle's folk gave us a room prepared with a clay stove, excited to have the new-married among them. We climbed the stairs with a candle, and all their eyes were on us. Then at last the door shut.

I had my bride, all mine in the eyes of the law and her family, and before God, as had been. Rosette Cordelia—now Churchill—has a fine name and a fine figure, fine light eyes and shining hair. Now we can cast off the troubles between us, now that we are wed. I could see care lifting from her all the day. She fairly glowed at her folks', all big smiles and twirling about like a girl.

Rosette was of two minds as we stood in that bedroom with the door shut—shy as she knew she was supposed to be, and eager as I knew she was. She delights when she has her way, but I am ready to be done with all this show. We spent a while kissing and holding, sitting on the side of the bed and sinking into the down quilt spread across it. Her hair was pulled smooth over her ears and looped up in a knot at the back. She unpinned her hat and set it on the table, and I unpinned her hair. It fell loose over the dark stuff of her dress and changed her altogether. With a low sound she dropped her arms and closed her eyes for me to begin all the unbuttoning and unwrapping. She helped with some of it—mysteries! My clothes were quicker to shift, and we rolled into the bed all in one motion, legs tangled, rightfully there at last. All bare, both of us, at last. Not much sleep before our journey, but no matter.

First thing the next morning, as she braided her hair, I walked back to her folks' for the new cutter. We got off late morning with two guests with us as far as Ionia, on our long way. We would have ten days alone but for the homes we would visit. As we pulled west out of town, my wife leaned up against me and held my arm, resting her head in its bonnet and shawl against my shoulder. I turned her chin up to see me, smiled down at her and asked, "Well, Mrs. Churchill, how do you fare today?"

"I fare well, Mr. Churchill—husband," she answered. "I hardly feel the cold, with the hot brick at my feet and the rugs you brought us. Do you know?" she asked, quiet over the shushing of the cutter in the snow. "I wrote this morning of our wedding, and of you."

"What did you say of me, then?"

"That I hope it will ever be as it is with us now, that I can make your life calm and peaceful."

"Is that what I lack, do you think?" I asked, pushing against what she implied.

"Well, no, but I want to bring you rest, and a sweet home."

"It will be a while for the home," I answered. "But by summer we should have one."

"And in the meantime we will have each other, be with each other, no matter where we are. At Father and Mother's, at Uncle Myron's and Aunt Lucinda's. How odd it is for me today to call them that, when yesterday they were Mr. and Mrs. King."

"I would rather have my own place, but it is well that we are married now," I said.

"Yes!" She squeezed my arm, then felt about in her bag for some cake her mother had packed for us.

The day was a fine one, and we made good time. The trees flashed past almost in rhythm, the river below us narrowing to just a bit that flowed between the icy banks. About three we arrived at the first house, my Uncle Arza King's. He was himself off to Kalamazoo with his family. His house was nearly a hotel, with boarders and some hired girls. Three King brothers have married three Garter sisters, Mother's younger ones, though one has died.

"Did they all love one another just so neatly, in pairs?" Rosette asked, when I gave her the history.

"I would not know that," I said. "But I have not heard of complaints."

"I suppose the cousins all look like brothers and sisters," she said.

"Could be."

I tended the horses and surveyed the premises—good construction of the stalls, but an inconvenient way with the troughs. Then I got back in the place and carried our bags up. I found her tucked up at a little desk by the window in our room, scratching away. This was her first chance to catch up with her book.

I hope she doesn't say much in there that someone might read, especially about before.

"Otis, did you see the girl with bloomers like mine?" she asked. No, I hadn't noticed.

Next day we got off only after dinner, nearly past one, and toward Uncle Henry Garter's, about six miles west of Grand Rapids and twenty-three miles from the Flat River. The cutter is a sound one, Ramsdell's horses beauties, and swift. We just skim along the river, throwing up showers of soft powder, crunching through the crust. Rosette tells me she wrote, *Our road lay along the bluffs of Grand River. A very pleasant country it is and prospering finely.* And the railroad will bring even more prosperity and people—they work it in various places along our route. She pressed my knee to stop us at the two long covered bridges. The one at the Rapids is the longest either of us has ever crossed—just three cents toll there while the other is six, near the junction of the Thorn Apple. We had our dinner at the Lake Tavern, and an old woman came in with a dull daughter.

"Please, sir," she asked the proprietor, talking like a woman in a book, "I have not means to pay, but need a place tonight. I am searching for my son, who I suppose is in the state somewhere. We can sweep or do some mending if you have need of that."

"No need," he answered. "You may stay here, but I have only the benches in this room, if those will do."

"Oh, we are grateful, but perhaps we would be better elsewhere."

I went out then, but Rosette told me the old woman wished Rosette's "brother," as she called me, could carry them back a half mile to a farm house she had seen. She told the old woman we were in a hurry, and so we were.

We passed Grand Rapids at dusk. It is a fine city with the last of the sun gleaming on the dark buildings and snow-covered roofs. The day froze into the dark with the wind, and my wife was chilled through—we needed to find Uncle Henry's. Four miles on the west side we inquired at a tavern for Henry Garter's place and had missed the turn, so it was only after several more miles and a few stops for help that we got there. I left her in the sleigh, as the house was dark.

I crunched up to the door and knocked, then found they were abed. Uncle Henry, a bear of a man, pulled me in. He threw a blanket around his shoulders, shoved his feet into his boots, and went out for Rosette. All of a sudden I was in the front room with a view straight into the room where Aunt was in the bed trying to pull on some clothes. I turned to look toward the door where Uncle had gone.

It soon burst open again with a kick and a wind-curl of snow—"Marian!" Uncle boomed. As he stood in the doorway with Rosette in his arms, he announced, "This is our new niece Rosette Churchill, Otis's bride."

"Well, set her down, then, Henry," she said, waiting until he did. "Glad to make your acquaintance, dear girl," she answered, stepping out of the bed into her slippers and extending a hand. "Let's us ladies stir up the fire to make a supper." Rosette caught herself right up in the spirit, and we soon held steaming cups and a bite to eat. It was hard to tell with just the firelight and a candle or two, but everything seemed in pleasant order. They soon found us a bed we fell into gratefully, and I scarcely knew where I was when I woke.

The next days we stayed with them, Uncle showing me around his good, new house, though Ramsdell's is more to my taste, with rooms to spare. He told me this town is called Walker now, and many are growing fruit trees here—peach and apple are well suited to the sandy soil.

Rosette went visiting some with Aunt Marian. They are light-hearted folk but somewhat slack—Uncle's trees are not ordered well and I worry for his hay stores and told him so. I showed him what Ramsdell has done to waterproof one side of his barn so the gales do not spoil the hay. He listened and let me do that for him, so I feel we've paid our keep.

My bride and I did not have much time alone, but there was no help for it. She used her good manners with all the people we met. We had been married five days when, one morning, we set out for Uncle Clinton Garter's, Mother's brother. I heated a couple of bricks to put at Rosette's feet, and she tucked herself in, still and tight. The cutter creaked down as I strode up into my place and grasped the reins. I tipped my hat to Uncle Henry and to Aunt Marian, behind in the doorway, and clicked my tongue—"Chick-chick." The horses—a-tremble to be off—flicked their ears and one ducked his head a bit. Their withers strained beneath the harness. We were hung up a bit on the ice, or a drift. But another "chick-chick" and twitch of the reins, another pull of the beast, and we lumbered forward, then slid, then glided—and away!

Three miles along to the west we passed the village of Berlin, with five corners, not the four we usually know. With more settlements growing every year, I suppose we will see more of these—Uncle Clinton told us later of a six-corners not far from him there.

Uncle Clinton and Aunt Harriet have a busier house, with children, mischief-makers like the ones back at

Ramsdell's. Rosette told me she likes Uncle's looks and says she hopes I look like him at his age. He is a fine man, and his wife a busy one. I hope Rosette will be of that sort. So much company came there at all hours of the day—a Birdsall to trade, a Perkins to sing, Aunt Harriet's brother Alonzo Van Gordon to supper. And we enjoyed a fiddle— Uncle plays nearly as well as Solomon. One night he played us a Stephen Foster song that Rosette wrote down:

> *Down on the Mississippi floating*
> *Long time I trabled on the way*
> *All night the cottonwood a toting*
> *Sing for my trulub all the day*
> . . .
> *Now I am unhappy and am weeping*
> *Can't tote the cotton wood no more*
> *Last night while Nelly was a sleeping*
> *Death came knocking at the door*
> . . .
> *Down in the meadow mong de clober*
> *Walked with my Nelly by my side*
> *Now all dem happy daze are ober*
> *Farewell my dark Virginny bride*

I have to allow that tune sticks, and I'll be humming it a long time to come:

Nelly was a lady. Last night she died.
Toll the bell for lovely Nell, my dark Virginny bride.[5]

---

[5] transcription in the journal, last two lines from Stephen Collins Foster, *Nelly was a lady: a beautiful Ethiopian melody* (New York: Firth, Pond, and Co., 1849). https://books.google.com

I can dance and sing in company if need be, to get along, but I mostly like a good tune for my work, chopping or sawing or hammering to the rhythm.

Uncle Clinton lives further west, not far to the lake from there, along the Grand. We did more visiting, and then went back to Uncle Harry's, with some good Madeira and nuts one night with another family, the Morgans . . . I think. Mrs. Morgan was a big fleshy woman running about to feed us. I was tiring of all this.

We then began to make our way home again with a day in Grand Rapids. Rosette gave me a miniature of herself when I courted her, and in the city I took her to pose for a full-length ambrotype.[6]

"I want it as a wedding present for us," I told her.

"But shouldn't you be in the image with me?"

"No, the bride is enough," I said. "And we can send it to Mother to show you to her, until we can bring her to us."

Near the establishment we saw a woman carrying a water pail on her head—likely Irish, her man working on the railroad. They live in shanties along the way. Too many, too much, too dirty. Give me clean woods and my own people.

The weather was good all along for our journey, but turning toward bitter cold. We were back at Uncle Arza's overnight, and Rosette pointed out the girl in those bloomers like hers—trousers, I say. I prefer a slim leg in a stocking, but those are not on offer to men's eyes in public—so bloomers or skirts makes no difference.

By the time we got to Uncle Myron's we were ready for a fire. We stayed in the room with the clay stove again, and Rosette was easier, more at home. She knows how I want her to be with me. I want her hair loose and flowing,

---

[6] a kind of photograph, successor of the daguerreotype

no corset but just a light gown in the cold, and dark, fine stockings, without the trousers. In summer we shall have less than that, especially when we have our own home. Until then, Uncle Myron has told us to come back to stay whenever we like—the room is usually free, and the company not so fraught as things are at Ramsdell's. I feel watched there.

* * *

And so I am back to work, under two weeks since we left, with horse and cutter restored to Ramsdell—who is now Father to me, I suppose. I began with chopping for that twelve dollars I had of Brower. At the end of a day I come back looking for some rest. It is so much infernal visiting all the time—people staying here, and Rosette going there. I am becoming known for my work, though. McKelvey had me grind an axe for him. Meanwhile the world is freezing more each day, winter closing on us like a fist. The snow shrinks down to squeak against my boots and flies off dry as I go about my work.

A precious few days we had the Ramsdell house alone to ourselves, but for Ellen and the boys, and played that it was ours. The Ramsdells took the new cutter to Lansing to have their portraits made in ambrotype, after seeing Rosette's, and bought the boys new boots. Then we learned that Uncle Myron intended to take his family on a journey and wanted us to keep house for them—we were eager to do it. No children, even. But still the people coming and going, and special care to be taken for the cold. McKelvey and another man joined us one night to huddle around the stove, and he importantly told us that a man somewhere hereabouts froze his hands, and another was so badly frozen that his arms and legs had to be amputated. Fools cannot keep themselves from harm, and these must not have taken the man's way of due care.

"Oh, Otis!" called Rosette to me that night in bed, after we slept a while. "I had a terrible dream!"

"What's that?" I mumbled, curling around her. So many dreams.

"We were traveling on foot, going down a steep hill, and I was ahead—"

"Not likely," I said into the back of her neck.

"Now don't make fun, Otis! This was terrible!"

"Go ahead, then."

"Well, I came to a chasm yawning at the bottom, an immensity of depth. I called you to see, to help. But just as you got there it disappeared and the hill just continued on as it should."

"So what does that tell you?" I asked.

"That you will take care of all the terrible things ahead, I suppose," she answered.

"That's right."

"But that wasn't all. After that we found a path leading left and a road leading right. We took the path. But Otis, that wasn't the right one! We soon found we'd taken the wrong way and had to retrace our steps. Then we took the road," she said.

I made light of it: "West to Grand Rapids, then. Were we to work on the railroad?"

"No, Otis. You mock me, and I was frightened."

"Well, if you just go my way, all will be well," I told her, turning over.

"I hope so," she said. She pulled the bedclothes closer around her, drawing me against herself. The clay stove crackled with its warmth, and we had our own. The world solidified outside, ice like rocks.

*From the Journal of
Rosette Churchill
February 1857*

Thursday 5th. *Rained most all day, & everything is covered with ice. We staid at Aunt's till after dinner & then came home. Otis staid all night, of course, as he always will if he can, as this is his home till he builds his house, for which he is now cutting logs to draw to the mill.*

Friday 27th. *Father went to Portland. Sol played for a party at Mr. A Stanton's in the evening. Mary staid there all night. . . . I dreamed that Diana had been buried about six months. Mother had a chest that she brought from Aunt Susan's & in it were each of us a bonnet trimmed in mourning.*

Sally - Thaw

HE NEW COUPLE HAVE BEEN back proper
for a couple of weeks now. They seem to be
faring well, pulling away from us and into each
other as it should be. Much as I am used to comings and
goings here, I keep feeling a little surprised each time I
meet Otis in the house. He is not easily folded into our
ways, however well he works with Jacob.

The other night, so it was, we set up for dominoes in
the front room, now clear of the cutter, thanks be. Each
knew the way of the thing—who goes next, Frank's little
feint with a piece or two for under the table. But Otis
missed the spirit of it somehow, and bit at Frank for
spoiling the game. Rosette laughed large to make nothing
of it, but we all felt the chill. In any case, he shows busy-
ness to make his home, forever cutting and drawing logs
to his place. Rosette smiles quietly to herself in her place
with her needle.

They spent a week keeping house at the Kings' while
they were away, and I think that was good for all of us. It
was jolly for Jerome to have them back for his eighth

birthday. He watched all morning at the window, then shouted when he saw them trudging around the bend. I went to the window, then, and my heart stirred to see Rosette on Otis's arm, their heads bent together as they walked. At dinner, with my currant cakes iced for the birthday and hot cider for a party, Otis gave Jerome a little hatchet of his own. He made him promise to help him with his taps when it is time. That made me glad.

And it seems almost time—it is thawing and freezing again in turns, and we even heard thunder with rain the other day. We are restless here, waiting for that work to begin, when everyone throws in for the sugaring. I began to fret at Solomon gone so long to Grand Rapids, but his letter eased my heart. It seems his pony Lady fell through a stable floor and injured herself so she could not stand for a while, delaying his return for a week. He came home today, on foot of all things, and I rushed out when I saw him. "Where is your pony? Is she well?"

"Well enough, Mother, but I traded her for a wagon."

"But why are you walking? You could have frozen!"

"Perfectly warm, Mother. But I could stand a bit closer to the stove, if I might," he smiled, ducking into the kitchen.

"Of course! And have some gingerbread, too." I followed, taking his wet cap and coat as he shed them. Sol settled before the stove, mouth wide to shove in the cake, his eyes crinkling as a sign that he would continue in a moment.

He finished the first big bite and said, "Fine gingerbread. Thank you."

"Very welcome, I'm sure," I said. "Now go on . . ."

"So the wagon I traded Lady for is a fine one, a two-horse! I left it until I arrange for the horses."

"Two?! Well, isn't that fine—how will you manage it?" I handed him a cup of hot milk, and he blew and sipped, then pushed back his chair from the stove a little.

"Well, I am not concerned. I can do it when I find the right horses, for the right price. But I thought it prudent to think ahead, to what I will need a year or two from now—something bigger than a pony."

"That's wise, Son. Being willing to walk in the meantime helps."

"And having Father's team to use at need, too!" he laughed.

Never mind I praised him, I worry and would speak of it. But Jacob would allow the young man his way without reproach. Perhaps it will be best after all.

Rosette and Otis have taken up Myron King's home as their own more than is ours, I think, because the other night they went over there and found everyone asleep. They crept up to bed, and no one knew they were there until morning. I could just see Lucinda's eyes wide at the rumble upstairs and having to count another few eggs for breakfast.

Rosette said, when they got back, "Mama, Mrs. King—Aunt Lucinda—has a cure for my hands!"

"What would that be?" I asked. I know Dr. Killey's salve has not been a help, and I have given up having the girl put her hands to any wet work, so painful and itchy her sores have been.

"One tablespoonful of tar, to three of lard, boiled in a pan of water for two hours. I am to put it on and then put on an old pair of gloves."

"I cannot see you doing that with your hand work—"

"But at night I could, in bed."

"Yes, in bed," I answered, smiling to think of the bride awaiting her groom there, done up in gloves as for a ball or to dig in the kitchen garden.

Strangers have been here of late, including three men working twenty acres nearby, who have built a shanty and called here for fire. I shiver to think of them in that mean place, but the quarters are close enough they can warm each other. One day we served a more eminent guest at breakfast, a white-haired sage who will speak this Friday and Saturday at the school house. Our men went off to tap thirty or forty trees and I was left to entertain this guest, and I could not for the life of me remember his name! I spoke to him of this and that, hoping for the others to return soon. When Jacob came in early, as the sap was not yet running, I caught the man's name but have lost it again just as quickly.

The men were full of a story at supper that night. It is fateful that the very axe Otis sharpened for McKelvey has chopped a tree that fell on Otis's steer! Jerome piped out the "thwok" of the axe and the creak and crash of the tree through the branches, then the soft grunt as it landed on its mark. Otis reddened to bear the loss and the pity of it once again in the telling. Jacob was silent, leaving Solomon to speak a friend's words of consolation. It would have been too much to bear from Jacob.

Thinking of fate, some of those very bridges in Grand Rapids that Rosette admired have now gone off with the biggest freshet anyone here has ever known. The bridge at Lyons is gone, as well, which hurts us most. The coldest winter, the heaviest floods—disaster on disaster. And we have our own to boot—again at the hands of Mr. McKelvey, or at his responsibility. Mr. McKelvey is a hearty, good man, but not always the most practically useful on a place. While we were all at dinner, his oxen tipped over a barrel that held syrup enough for a full one-hundred twenty pounds of sugar! Oh, the waste of it!

But we sugared off over sixty pounds in any case, a good start. Jacob left our boys to run the boil today while he went to Portland. Rosette and I had the house quiet, having sent the boys' dinner out with them to the sugar-bush. I have not heard her dreams of late—perhaps she tells them to Otis? Is there anything to credit to those symbols, if the dreamer does not know the symbols herself? Cousin Betsy holds it so. And it is a way to know Rosette's thoughts, so I asked her, to see what we might auger from them.

"Have you dreams these days?" I asked as we rolled yarn together. The wool rubs her hands, but the wool oil soothes.

"Well, yes, but I don't know . . ." She rested the moss-green tangle in her lap.

"Have you one that troubles you?"

"More that it might trouble you, Mama—about Diana."

"Oh," I answered, with a pang, and idly wrapped one strand about my forefinger. Diana. Twenty she would be just now, and more my own self than is Rosette, who knows it. "It is no matter. Did she speak to you?"

"No, Mama. You know I do not hold with that idea, of speaking from the grave. My dream was about our mourning, though."

I nodded my head for her to go on, suppressing a sigh.

"Well, Diana had been buried about six months," she hesitated . . .

"Very well. Go on." I thought of how I'd dragged myself through those days, spending many of them abed, nursing Baby Frank when they brought him to me. I left Rosette to carry the women's work on her own. Jerome was so little and needing me, and Ellen was his little mother. Dark days. I spread my fingers across my lap, bracing myself a little.

"You went to Aunt Susan's and came back with a chest—it was like one in our room at Uncle Myron's. That must be where I got the thought of that chest from. There's a key always stuck in the lock—Aunt Lucinda keeps old ribbons and a baby dress and some Valentines in it. I looked."

"I'm sure you did!" I laughed, and was glad for it.

"In any case, you brought the chest in the house and opened it to show a bonnet for each of us. They were trimmed in mourning, with narrow white ribbon. And there were some pretty little hats," she said.

"Of course hats!"

"On our bonnets were rich, black crape veils, and for each of us a mourning collar, plain white."

"We didn't have those then," I said.

"No," she said slowly, and we sat quietly, remembering. In those days she had no time to sew proper mourning for us with all the work to do. Mine takes all of each day, and a girl on her own . . . "No, we did not," she said again.

"But you did the work well, as I recall," I said, not really remembering at all.

"Glad to get back to my proper work when you were better," she smiled. "In the dream we knew that these things were there some time and we had forgotten them. I asked you if we could wear them, and you said yes."

"Too late to do so now, with all that has passed," I told her. "But it would have been pleasant to have those pretty, sad things at the time."

"I don't know—perhaps it is better to just move on, put the sadness behind us. Do the next cheerful thing." She tucked the ball of yarn into her basket.

"Or perhaps we can see in this dream," I answered, "a message that we would do well to be prepared for the sad and difficult. Then we are not so crippled by them when they come."

"I hope . . ."

"Yes," I matched her. "I hope we have no need." No need of fancy mourning in the soon-coming days.

The last day of Mary White's school came around, and Sol went with me to visit overnight at the Kings'. When I opened the bag I found I had taken Rosette's nightdress and cap, which must have been on the bed when I bundled my things. Sometimes I fear I bustle about like a foolish hen, clucking and scratching. It is good to be alone with my boy for a bit, he to squire me along. He has been spending time with Miss White, but I do not believe she is the one to be his wife, though she is good as he is good.

"What do you think of the principle from Professor Gregory that the student must love learning in order truly to learn?" Solomon asked her as they cleared the supper table together. I cocked an ear to listen. I could almost hear her blushing and dipping her head as she murmured some little nothing and then spoke a little louder.

"Well, I don't know how many do love what they learn," she said, her voice low. "But I hope they learn in any case."

They almost speak past each other. He delves into matters of policy in the school board and theories he reads in *The Journal of Education*. She smiles but is content to recite simple poems with the children. She dances prettily as he plays, but wanders out of the room if he begins a piece she cannot dance to.

From the Journal of
Rosette Churchill
March 1857

    Tuesday 31st. Went with Otis in the morning to the sugar-bush. Got back just at sun down. Came by our folks' bush & they were sugaring off. Ann & Cornelius, Mrs. Martha White, & Maria & Mianda Martin were there, so we put down our sugar & joined the party. We sugared off 28 lbs, making in all 203 for us, & our folks 118, making for them 705. We have all finished working in the bush, except to make vinegar. Cloudy & warm.

Rosette - Sugar-Bush

*O*TIS WAS UP AND DRESSING, creaking the ropes as he sat on the bed. I forced open my eyes, groaning at the sleep still heavy upon me. He thundered through the door as I lay on my side gazing dully toward the bedside table. There stood a dish with a puddle of black from the guttered candle. On the floor, its yellow covers split apart, lay *The Black Avenger of the Spanish Main*, finished with the last hiss and waver of the candle as sleep overtook us last night. On the frozen winter nights the story warmed us—the sea and pirates and sultry climes, another world from ours. It was cold and still outside our room, and outside the house, where our work waits for us.

Most evenings now we have callers, and Clarinda Howe is my cheerful shadow, learning the hand-work. After a very cold but sunny day we enjoyed an evening here with several men. Nancy and Elsie Utter made with me and Clarinda our work party after dinner, and I set most all of my love-knot bed quilt together. Daytime we worked by the windows in the front room, the southerly sunshine low in the sky across the panes all day. Our voices were like those of birds—soft and cheerful and light. In the evening the men were more like dogs, barking and growling a little and not minding me on the other side of the room with my darning. Their smoky pipes and wet leather filled the house with the smell of men. Darkness and cold draw us all in toward the stove and its glow.

Next day Clarinda and I returned the visit to Elsie in the afternoon, then Sol and Otis and I walked through softening snow and trees dripping with the day's warmth to the McKelveys'. With steady industry and long patience, Otis helped Colonel make sap-boughs, as he is making sugar himself. The three of us encouraged the luckless McKelvey in the work, as if he were a child. His trees promise abundant yield, and it would be too bad for him to miss by poor care the opportunity of the sugar.

The maples, silent keepers of their secret among all the green trees, flame out their place in fall that we might find them. Then in the leanest time of year, when all the harvest stores have dwindled, they provide well. With careful watching they yield good sugar for all of us. The Indians have been saved from perishing some late winters with the sap straight from a tree. It is only the barest hint sweet, but has given life for all that, if the stories are true. An Indian visited here only days ago, standing quiet on the doorstep of the kitchen until Mother saw him. He bought a pound of sugar of Father. Dozens of quarts went into that, patiently tapped from many trees, transformed to sugar with our pans and fire.

Otis has supplied himself two patent pails and a tin dipper from Portland. Then he went to Ionia on foot for a fifteen-pound sheet of iron, two dollars, to make himself a pan with Father's help. Sol has been traveling about to see to getting some cows—he stayed somewhere we know not for two days and returned with a white and a red cow for fifty dollars.

Meanwhile I am here by the fire, making the outside of another bed quilt out of three of my delaine[7] dresses. As I handle each one I remember days I spent wearing it, knowing those days are gone. Days with Timothy in Kalamazoo, teaching my school. The dance when I was new to all eyes there. Even the day I first saw Otis on our doorstep welcoming me to my own house! But one day we will spread ourselves with the quilt-yet-to-be when we have our own bedstead in our own house. We might be tucked in with the babe-yet-to-be. My thoughts then can cast back to those days as I touch each square or diamond, the feel of each conjuring up a time since past.

When our babe is grown and we are old, will I tell those stories as I hold a grand-child's finger against one square, then another? Only a little child will listen, or a bookish girl. Most men and boys care only for the warmth, quilt upon quilt, the stories hidden. Otis reads to me of an evening, though, when we have quiet. Those nights at Uncle Myron's were ours alone, for reading of the Avenger, and Fanny Campbell. Father and Sol insist, at home, on high-minded works from Father's library—or political essays in the newspapers—not the bright new paper-cover books from Lyons and Ionia. "Passing trash," Sol calls them with a smile, and Daddy nods.

A day or two after mid-month I took our supper to Otis's sugar-bush, and we ate by firelight, no candle. It was our first supper at our own place. The next evening we had an adventure that I wrote up in my journal. I know I'll tell of it for years to come, when our own children are learning to sugar off as Sol and I learned first, as now the boys and Otis learn with my parents:

---

[7] spelled "delane" in the journal, a high-quality woolen fabric

Friday 20th. I went to Otis' bush towards night to help bring up the sugar that was left the night before. He boiled till eleven. He got the big chair up in front of the fire, which is made of the end of an old stove-trough. There was one hole in the back, but he put a board on it & it makes a nice warm chair, & there I sat & dozed as easily as a kitten.

We started with torches to come home, but in crossing a swail,[8] in which I wet both feet completely, we got off the path, the torch went out, & all his efforts to relight it were vain. So we wandered on without any path or anything to guide us, till we were tired of walking. I told Otis we should have to stay out all night. He thought not. And O such walking! Brush, sticks, boggs, logs, & holes, had to be successively surmounted, & as we were going, I noticed a black stripe of ground before us, but thought it was only bare of leaves till Otis was walking a wee creek. He told me to get on his back & he would take me over. I put one arm round his neck & with [the] other I held fast to my six quart pan full of sugar & he set me across. We walked on, but no signs of any place.

We retraced our steps across the rivulet & soon came to the stream running across the south side of the farm, into which he stepped but [he] having me by the right hand, I escaped & seated myself on a knoll on which I walked on the roots of some saplings that overhung the brook, while he lighted a match & found by the current that we were going the wrong way. We again turned back, & coming to a large log seated ourselves thereon & staid I should think about an hour, but could not tell by my watch as it was so dark I could not see. Then as it grew some lighter we started & coming to a flat that was bare ground we concluded to stay there till morning.

---

[8] swale, a low-lying area of land, usually damp

My feet had grown so cold I was afraid they would freeze, so taking off my shoes & shawl, Otis wrapped the latter about them, & took them into his lap till they were warm. Then he put a small stick by the side of a tree, & after having been there half an hour, looked at my watch and found it was only 20 minutes past two. O misery, we were so cold & long it would be till morning. As we sat on the big log we would peer out into the dark to see if we could not catch the glimmer of some light or the sound of some voice. But no. All was still. Not a dog, or cow-bell, or goose was to be heard. Sometimes we would fancy we could hear somebody talking, but soon found it to be only the moaning of the wind, or the creaking of a tree, so we seated ourselves on our rude seat & getting close together waited the coming morning, & I actually slept most all the time notwithstanding the cold. We aroused up once in a while & stamped around to keep our feet from freezing, or rather I did, & there we staid put till morning. And that was the first night we staied on our own home.

Saturday 21st. As soon as day began to break, we started for home, & soon came to the place where we lost the way, & then we walked on quite cheerily, but my feet were so benumbed I could hardly keep myself upright. I hit every stick that came in my way & was sure to go astride all the bushes I met, & when I got home my dress & cloak were in tatters.

To look back at these words I see fun and sweetness in Otis warming my feet, and he was at his best in doing that. But the words do not convey how awful it felt at the time—the desperation of cold, the fear beginning in my heart, the terrible aloneness out there in the dark. And how we quarreled at finding the way. I can hear my fractious voice and his impatience with me, not wanting to be reminded we were lost.

In the end, all was well, and Otis has made a good start on his sugar-making. Even late in the season he was tapping more trees. One day I went to Howes' to get the neck yoke for him to carry more and stayed to supper with Clarinda. Mrs. Howe was sugaring off in the house, sending up clouds of steam that eased my lungs and softened my tight, dry face. It was the best sugar I have ever tasted. Perhaps the small amount in the pan gets special care with a woman's touch that the big pans outdoors do not.

"So, Rosette, how do you fare these days with your new husband, and your home things?" Mrs. Howe asked me as she stirred the syrup.

"Faring well, Mrs. Howe, and enjoying Clarinda's company with the hand-work."

"Do I understand from your mother that you already expect a child?"

"Yes," I answered, sitting up straighter to draw in my figure. "Fall—"

"October, I should hope," she returned, looking sharply at my waist. Clarinda bent her head over the button she was sewing onto a cuff.

"Or a little earlier," I replied. "Mother says she has always tended toward the early babes, and smaller."

"In any case, Rosette, you will need to care for yourself," she smiled. "We're almost to the sugar—just a moment or two."

"Thank you, I will. I have such a taste for green things, and nothing yet green to eat, but some leeks we had just this week. I could have eaten them all, with the children, but the men didn't like them, so we left off. We went out fishing but caught none—wouldn't fish taste good just now?"

"Oh, yes," sighed Clarinda. "And a cup of berries . . ."

"Soon enough," Mrs. Howe replied. "Everything is beginning to stir for spring."

I trudged home with the yoke across my shoulders—the easiest way to carry it. I thought how good it was to help my husband, to enter into his labors. But when I arrived he was silent as he took it from me and started straightway to the wood, leaving me purposeless in the yard.

* * *

Such long days of the sugaring off. Some days they start by late morning and are not done until almost midnight. It all depends on the quantity, the strength of the fire, the wind, everything. My folks keep getting eighty or ninety pounds at a time, one day one-hundred twenty-seven. Otis makes less, but it is a start. In the last days of the month we have tallied up our sugar. With the end of the work, our folks have gotten almost four times what Otis has, but he is already planning for next year to increase his yield. "I need bigger pans to boil in," he said as we prepared for bed last night. "If I could get help to drain more trees, if I had one of those compartment arrangements like your father's . . ."

"All in good time, Otis," I answered. "You cannot have everything at once."

From the Journal of
Rosette Churchill
April 1857

    Tuesday 14th The snow was two inches deep in the morning, but disappeared before night. The snow was light & hung on the trees so that they did look beautiful, as though they had been dressed in the finest plumes of white feathers.

Rosette - Domestics

R. AND MRS. MCKELVEY are welcoming me at their home now to board, since the sugaring is done. Otis is at Uncle Myron's, so we are closer together while he builds his house, but still apart. I can just see the corner of the Kinneys' house from my bedroom window here, and from the other side of their house I can just see the chimney of Uncle Myron's. It's no far walk in the summer, but when we labor through the snows or mud, it is more than I can think of, so weary. This is a good house that Otis helped Mr. McKelvey raise, and I know we will have one this good or better in time—Otis is always working for the one thing further, the one thing finer.

I walked home through the quiet snows yesterday to get some of my clothes, while Otis went to Ionia to buy some things for our home. I am stouter now, my corsets at the end of their laces, so I tie them firm but not cinched as before. I must let out another dress or two soon. Along the road I went, fat white flakes swirling about me. The trees sifted down the snow more lightly as the branches caught the white that piled up on their backs.

At home Mother was wrapping pounds of sugar for those who stop to buy of us—or them, I should say. Little Frank ran to pull at my mittens and put them by the fire to dry. With Jerome out working with Father, and Ellen off to some house or other, Frank does not know his place. We are two of a kind. Mama seemed glad and unsurprised to see me, but she is busy about her own work and paid me little heed.

So I agreed to read to Frank a while—*The Mariner's Library*. We sat by the stove and I took him on my lap, and I could feel my cheeks grow red from the fire after red from the cold outdoors. He impatiently turned to the pages of pictures—"Bird Catchers" and "The Pirate's Treasure," and wanted me to read the latter. "For the pirates were resolute and reckless." But I turned instead to "The Ocean," by Hawthorne:

> Calmly the wearied seamen rest
> Beneath their own blue sea.
> The ocean solitudes are blest,
> For there is purity. [9]

His finger traced the words with mine—he is a quick one for five! I could almost teach him to read if I had the time.

Father and Jerome came in for dinner, which I helped Mother lay on the table. Sol and Charley stomped in from

---

[9] Nathaniel Hawthorne, "The Ocean," in *The mariner's library or voyager's companion: Containing narratives of the most popular voyages from the time of Columbus to the present day... and illustrated by fine engravings.* (Boston: C. Gaylord, 1834), 34. https://books.google.com

their own work just as we sat down. Mother expected callers for the afternoon, bringing Ellen home, and I wanted to be solitary. I made my goodbyes and set out. I heard the ladies' chatter as they approached from the north. I waved my hand, nearly dropping my bundle, and shouted a greeting.

At the McKelveys' Ann exclaimed at my return, eager to show me the open-work basket she'd been finishing for me. It is a gift. She is so good to me—as Diana was—and I do not well return her care, as stiff as I can be. But perhaps her warmth and goodness will seep into me while I live here in her cordial company. Father named me Cordelia with that warmth in mind, I expect, but got it only with Diana. I am Rosette—Mother chose that name. I am tight and prim, not wide open with welcoming love. Even with Otis, I answer his vigor with my own firmness, not yielding and soft. Our love is fierce and quick. Daddy is very proper with Mama in our seeing, but I have seen him tender with her. He uses a voice he thinks we do not hear or a touch he thinks we do not see, and she leans in to him with the tiniest smile.

Married folks are a curiosity to me. Some young couples carry on just as they were before, nothing changed between them or with others. I suppose Otis and I seem that way. I am drawn into his plans, doing my part. My attention is toward him and his business, and he turns his purposes to my work, to direct it and supply it. He brought me from Ionia three rolls of batting and eight yards of calico, so that I can begin to make bedclothes. It is simple work, the cutting and hemming, and much is finished quickly. Then I lay it in store for our home. The batting disappears inside the quilts but gives them substance, weight, and warmth.

Is it enough just to tend to these things, for purpose and some beauty? Is it enough to fashion a life of making and mending and forever washing and drying?

Ann and Colonel McKelvey, as he wants to be called—simpler than "Cornelius"—have a life together that is a pleasure, despite his hopelessness with farming. He bumbles, and she smiles. He confesses another accident, and she comes in under his arm, her own about his waist to support him. He fairly glows with it. Otis has mishaps of a different kind. He slashes himself regularly with his blades, but works along so fast and hard that it doesn't stop him for long. Neither of us has Ann's patience . . . nor Colonel's sweetness, for that matter. We can learn of them.

The men are logging, drawing up the lug-way to the mill, and piling up lumber for our place—it is exciting to think of it! How my thoughts cast about—one new thing after another.

* * *

We were all back at Mother and Father's for Sunday dinner, McKelveys included. In the afternoon Colonel went to the nurseryman and Otis would boil in some sap for vinegar—always working! We ladies visited in Mama's south room, enjoying the spring sunshine between the snows. If it stayed clear, Ann and I would wash together on Monday—as in the nursery rhyme. I expected, though, that she would do most of the work and I would do a little. I am weary with this babe, though I feel my strength returning.

Monday we began our work week again, and it was good to see how Ann does her washing. I never really paid much attention at home before Diana died and I had it all to do while Mother was ill. But I do not do much washing of late—with my own work to do and my poor hands. Ann soon felt sorry for me and sent me out with some mother[10] for our vinegar barrel. Meantime she finished the washing and got it inside, and I had just returned when the rain started, becoming snow later on. Mother and Uncle Myron visited through the afternoon, and Ann boiled down some syrup to make wax[11] for us. Tuesday morning we woke to a fairy snow, blown away with a tremendous wind on Wednesday. That made Otis remember he'd left his mittens at Keefer's mill last week.

Our days settle into a small circle of visitors here and at their homes. Otis called one day and we went together to the Kinneys', where he left me as he went on to the Kings'. He came back for supper with me and then walked me back to the McKelveys'. Round and round we go. But soon enough we will be planted on our own place and folk can come to visit us. Otis brought me a fine paper his brother Sylvester sent him, *The True Flag*. Some women writing in it seem quite fierce—I do not know anyone like them. Whirled up with the abolition is the idea that women ought to own property, and then have a vote as well. Would Otis's place then be our place? And when would I have time to learn enough to know how to vote? It is too much to think of.

Father called and invited us to dinner as he passed along on some errand, and later, after Sol stopped here for a drink during his work, he walked along with us. My brother and my husband are not easy with each other, and I have lost something of my old banter with Sol. I felt pressed down by the quiet. After our dinner, Mother came back with me, and we saw the first snake of the year. No

---

[10] a term for the culture added to a juice to ferment it into vinegar

[11] a maple candy made like taffy, hardened on a bed of snow

time for work, but I have already set together a couple of comforters and quilts.

I awoke next morning with teeth-ache and suffered until Otis brought me some oil of cloves from Uncle Myron's. While I waited for him I repented the wax I've eaten so much of lately, that sticks in my teeth. But the oil of cloves relieved it so I could work with Ann on my quilt, and I will help her with hers next. She thought it would be fun to go to the Howes' and fetch Aunt Lucinda along the way, but she was too busy to go with us. She did ask if we'd take little Marian and Henry along to my parents' place, so we made a parade of it. A sudden headache put me in bed all afternoon while we were visiting the neighbors, so that I had to stay in a strange house overnight, but Otis came and stayed with me.

Oh, such visiting—half a dozen ladies here to see Ann and me in one afternoon, in two groups that all stayed together until I could feel my headache coming on again. But as I am indisposed, I can retreat to the bedroom when it is too much for me. And then five of them were back two days later, when we also entertained Otis's Cousin Churchill Garter, just here from New York. He stayed for supper. The two of them went next day to Lyons and Ionia, and a day after that to the nurseryman, and brought home currant, cherry, and plum sprouts we are to plant. All during this visiting I went easy and read for the second time, *Thinks-I-To-Myself*:

> I was born of very honest, worthy, and respectable parents: at least I think so. They were certainly fully as much so as their neighbours: their circumstances were affluent; their rank in life conspicuous; their punctuality as to the discharge of all just debts, and regular payment of their trades-people, unexceptionable. They generally appeared to be regarded by all around them in a very respectable

light, being in the habit of receiving and returning, according to the customs of the world, all the usual compliments and civilities of visits, entertainments.[12]

How do we compare, out here in this new frontier? We pay the visits and use fine manners, but we have no pavements to keep our feet clean, no shops around the corner to run to for an extra bun for supper if someone comes by. We have no cards to exchange in calling, and certainly no butlers at the door! Here children do for servants, and pioneer-spirit young people pay their way with labor. Otis chops his wood or Miss White keeps school—on sharp watch for an opportunity.

At his home the other night, Uncle Myron told of his own start: "I grew up helping my father with his shop. I rolled the barrels of meal up the ramp, made change for customers. With several sons, my father could leave the store to only one, but he meant to send us out to begin our own—Arza, Norton . . ."

"But you were not content inside a store, were you?" asked Aunt Lucinda, looking about at the children to be sure they listened.

"No," he laughed. "You know me well, Lucinda. Every time I pried open the top of a barrel to look inside, I could not help thinking back to how that dried corn got there, what size plot was needed to grow cucumbers for pickles enough to fill a barrel, and whence the vinegar and peppercorns would come to season it. I always cast back to the beginning . . . to the soil."

"And so we came here, and you have been happy as a lark," she smiled.

---

[12] Edward Nares, *Thinks-I-To-Myself: A Serio-Ludicro, Tragico-Comico Tale Written by Thinks-I-To-Myself Who* (New York: M.W. Dodd, 1843), 3. https://books.google.com

"The land suits me. But I don't know as I will stay here many more years. The hills to the northwest, nearer Grand Rapids, are lovely. And a farm can't prosper without custom—a solid town is needed."

Otis looked up then: "Do you not think Lyons is prospering, and Ionia, Uncle?"

"They might," Uncle Myron answered. "But with rivalries between Montrose[13] and Lyons, and all seeming to grow up without care of the farms, I don't know how they will fare in the days to come. They buy things off the river instead of from us, to start. But we are doing well enough now. And in the meantime, I build up this hundred and sixty acres to draw a buyer in case I want to remove."

Otis listened, his brows furrowed. Was he considering his own place and that we were just getting started? Myron King and Father have much to teach him, but he must find his own way. If he makes a farm as productive and beautiful as theirs, he will do well, and I.

In May will come my twenty-seventh birthday, and I am so much better set now than for my twenty-sixth. I have a husband, a farm beginning to be planted, a baby to be born soon. I have a settling of the most pressing questions I held in my heart at this time last year.

I lived last spring in fear and longing, having left behind Timothy and without Otis yet in sight. It was a perilous place for an aging maid, but I dared not speak of it aloud, though I know some whispered. But then came Otis, and a different kind of longing—and fear. How the storm clouds gathered in late fall as we rushed headlong to marriage, fearing to miss having all things decent and in order.

---

[13] the town later named Muir, just north of Lyons

But no matter now—I will celebrate the birthday by piecing for a bed quilt the nine of spades I have in mind. Mother tells me it would be best to consult Cousin Betsy on the figure, as she recalls something ill of that sign. But I refuse to hold with the Tarot and am satisfied with the plan. It is three by three, and seeming trees, the spade itself being a good symbol for a farmer. It makes no matter to Otis, insensible as he is to things of the spiritual realm. He does like "practical preaching," as he calls it. We are mostly of the same mind on that, but I wonder whether doing right is all that God requires. Can we, by doing some large part of things right, overshadow the things we have done wrong?

From the Journal of
Rosette Churchill
May 1857

Saturday 2nd. I went with Otis to his farm, to set out some
things.

Monday 4th. Cold & windy & cloudy all day. Jenette Watson
commenced her school. Rained all night.
Tuesday 5th. My 27th birth day. Stormy & cold with snow in the
morning.

Otis - Homestead

AFTER MUCH SICKNESS OF LATE, my wife bestirred herself to go to Kinney's for some horseradish root, as I prepared to plant, and Father Ramsdell returned from Grand Rapids with the summer schoolteacher. I was glad to take Rosette to our farm to do our first planting, setting out sixty-six currants—five of them white—nine plums, three cherries, and four horseradish roots. It is a start.

It is good to work the earth on my own place, my wife busy beside me. We went out to plant potatoes in the field I had plowed up with the ox. Rosette went before me dropping the pieces, and I scraped up the loose soil to cover them, Irish fashion. She does not like to muss up her skirts and boots—shoes, she calls them—and takes great care in the evenings cleaning them, when they'll only get dirty next day. But it helps her appearance, so that is good. As we worked I conjured up a picture in my mind of the farm as it will be—shanty first, back of the rise where the house will go, these fields, and a good barn. Then I will raise our house, squared up to the road but with two trees before to shield it from the snows and wind from the north. It will be backed up by the shanty, which can become our sugar store. Our kitchen door will face to the south for the sun and warmth in winter. Having our bedroom above the kitchen with a window to the east will make for hearty early mornings in summer, a quick start to our days.

I spoke of the house to Rosette, who straightened up from stooping over the potatoes and put her fist to her back to ease it, smiling at my plan and brightening with plans of her own, no doubt. I think she will wait to see what I do and then bend her doing to mine, as it should be. I bought her calico and batting, and she turned them into bedclothes now bundled up in a corner at McKelvey's. She lays in store the things she can make or get for our place, one quilt like a playing card and the one she works on now in stars. She makes them from dresses I have seen her wear. She economizes and proves herself as good as I thought she would be.

She is fairly round now with our child, and cannot bind her figure much to hide it. I don't like seeing her in others' houses, when we should by rights have our own, but we both work on it most days. She picked cowslips in the slough[14] the other day, exclaiming like a child over their being her first grass of the spring. I let her eat most of my portion, too. The green things are fine, but potatoes do me better for my work, and salted beef until we can have fresh again. Rosette does not seem to have much interest in the kitchen work at McKelvey's, never mind Ramsdell's, where her mother tends to all that. She must soon learn to cook, though, when our shanty is done.

We have been piling up quilts and sugar loaves and logs and the stones I have plowed up in my fields, in readiness. It is better to do things this way, I think, having

---

[14] a low, marshy area

the surety of our marriage to hold us together and places to lay our heads and have our board while we both work on our place. I could not well do all this work without the sometime comfort of her woman's body to ease me in the way. Solomon is building his house alone, without a woman yet chosen for it. That seems to me the wrong way about, when the woman can hold aloof and let the man shift for all that needs doing. Rosette was cool to me most times in the fall when I courted her, even when we knew our intentions, and her work seemed only for herself, not for me—all dresses and handkerchiefs. This is a better way—we are both sojourners from house to house, preparing our things, rather than only I seeming not to have a home.

Ann McKelvey shows my wife her womanly ways in baskets and wool yarn, and in the kitchen. Rosette asks her silly questions sometimes: "Ann, whatever do you do with all the grease?"

"Well, it depends what we might need it for," Ann replied. "The bacon and ham grease is good for cooking the next thing in the skillet."

"And I know the lard from the pot in the yard—we use that for soap."

"Yes, for there's little flavor in that," Ann replied. She is patient, seeing that in her mother's kitchen Rosette was blind to the goings-on, having taken little part in them. Just by doing what Ann does Rosette is learning without knowing it.

I have been spending time showing Cousin Churchill Garter our workings in the area, as he considers his own life to be made here, possibly. I am glad to have someone under me, newer than I, that I might set out my own plans to a willing student. Uncle Myron is known for his successes here, but I soon will be, I warrant, and Churchill knows that. He sees how I manage my wife and approves.

She is more sober than Aunt Lucinda, who is cheerful but dizzy sometimes with the visiting.

Rosette and I brought my ox to Uncle Myron's field the other day, she just for company and to invite Churchill to have supper with us at McKelvey's. Rosette was to make most of the meal, Ann to help. It made a good impression. They even made a cake to share with Solomon next day for his twenty-fourth birthday.

My wife's own birthday was to be a few weeks later, and her family makes much of birthdays. She presses me into their ways, and I played a good guest to give some trifle to Jerome on his birthday in December. But he is a child, and she grown. I did not give anything to Sol. Her mother's cake should be enough, and I hold firm to that.

* * *

As the month draws to a close, summer is coming. The planting has begun in earnest. Churchill and I planted corn for Uncle Myron until midafternoon, then came to McKelvey's to do the same. Suddenly around us the trees are greening up, but the mosquitoes are coming out, and Rosette is troubled by them. We took a walk in the warm evening breeze, away from the marshy land, and the mosquitoes were not so bad along the road. We saw a night rainbow, the second this week. The pale colors glowed near the crescent moon, and Rosette asked if I found them entrancing or ominous—ghostly. "Just curious," I told her. "Nothing more than a change of weather."

Next day Churchill left for New York again, to consider his plans, and I sent with him the ambrotype of Rosette for Mother to keep awhile and to show our friends.

Sol's dog Prince showed up here one day and would not go home, especially because it was Rosette trying to drive him, but Sol fetched him again in the evening. Next day Rosette and Ann had a time with McKelvey's calf that got out of its yard. She fairly collapsed with laughing to tell of Ann trying to steer it by laying hold of its tail, but Father Ramsdell and Sol happened along and put it back. And then in the long evening, after supper while I was away and not knowing of it, they took the women back to Ramsdell's house with them for a while. I missed seeing Rosette that night and then all next day, so I set off for Howe's, knowing that's where they'd gone for the day. I thought to meet them on their way home, but they were still visiting with the schoolteacher. They tried to get me to stay all night, noting the constant rain, but I had work to do and could not be bothered, so I went back. I did not like sleeping alone another night, and the soaking did not help matters.

Next day, as they told me, on their way home in the first sunshine for a week, they stopped to rest on a log by the road, and a crazy man went by, talking to himself. I don't know who might be about these days, with all the new ones coming in, but I don't like my wife out alone with whoever it might be—even the sticking plaster[15] peddler seems to warrant watching.

---

[15] an adhesive bandage

From the Journal of
Rosette Churchill
June 1857

    Friday 12th. Sol & Jenette started to go to Mr. Watson's to be gone till Sunday. Otis finished moving & as he forgot . . . to buy a broom, begun to make one out of a hickory stick.

    Saturday 13th. We came over in the morning, & mopped the shanty, fixed things round as well as we could, went to Mr. K's twice for some of our things, Otis went away in the afternoon to the letting of a job on the road & ate supper at fathers & we staid in our own house the first night & we are happy as larks, but the mosquitoes are thick enough to eat me up, & I can hardly write they act so. We have nothing else to trouble us now.

Solomon - Housekeeping

I HAVEN'T BEEN SEEING MUCH of Sister and Otis lately, while they've been at the McKelveys' and Kings'. They seem to be getting along alright, though impatient to get their shanty done. I'm freed up, now that planting is over, to do for them, and glad of it. I look for ways to improve on Otis's plans when I work my own place, working in hope. To judge of Otis and Rosette so shifted about from house to house, and peered at all the while as newly married, I mean to have a home first. I want to carry my bride to my own house our first days as man and wife, and show how I mean to keep and provide for her.

I do hope Jennette will have me. Something in me answers to her spirit when she is about, and her sweet smile pours sunshine into me. June is her month, she bending herself just a little toward each person with whom she has to do, as the wheat or hay bends supple with the wind, then springs back up into its soft place, ready to bow

again with the next breeze. But she is not like Pliable[16]—
she knows no variableness.

If we are to be man and wife, we will look ahead to our
children's children, to give them what we have been given,
a true heritage. Otis works without thinking beyond crops
and yields—he has little care for the cultivation of the
people he and Rosette will be together. At least he does not
discuss it with me in those long evenings on the porch as
he whittles and I muse. Rosette is a fine schoolteacher and
can teach their children their sums and reading and script,
but I want a wife who will see beyond those forms to the
things behind them. It comes to this: Rosette loves her
adventure novels, and Otis is willing to read them to her,
but Jennette pores over Spenser and discusses a bit of
Plato with Father.

"So, Mr. Ramsdell," she asked him one Sunday
afternoon. "Do you think Plato had knowledge of eternity
even without the Scriptures to tell him truly?"

Father raised his eyebrows at that and replied, "Do you
mean in the idea of true government, in the *Republic?*"

"Well, I don't know much of that, though I would be
privileged to read it," she answered. "But I was thinking of
the bit I read about the cave, and how what we see is only a
dim shadow of what is—"

"—And that we see in a mirror dimly now . . ."

"Yes!" she said. "And then face to face!" Both of their
faces were alight then, and I grew surer of claiming her for
my own.

But I have not everything in order. I can learn of Otis's
industry, but he pushes in anger, overloads, stretches the
things too far for their bearing. He is not stingy with
Rosette, though. He got Myron King to help him fetch a

---

[16] a character in John Bunyan's *Pilgrim's Progress*, known
for his susceptibility to persuasion

stove for the shanty, and it was just shy of thirty dollars. Rosette excitedly showed the goods he got for her—over thirty yards of factory cloth and four of toweling—for the new baby. Dishes for about four dollars, a work tub and washing board, thread, starch, tea, saleratus,[17] and some nails for the building—in all he spent almost forty-two dollars, the stove on credit. Just as Rosette finished showing me these things, Jennette called with Ellen—a nice surprise. We keep finding ourselves together, and I think neither of us minds at all.

Rosette has been able to keep house this week at the McKelveys' and was doing pretty well with the meals and all; Otis is drawing wood day by day, from the King place to Keefer's mill and back to his place, setting all in readiness. I saw him on the road when I paid Rosette a visit and took her to see a mule colt. "Oh, Sol, its ears are as long as my hand!" she cried. It's a pleasure to show her things. And now Father and Mother have asked her and Otis back to our house for the week, knowing they will soon be in their own shanty and Rosette confined. Rosette will then have work enough to keep her at home.

No sooner had Otis set out from here Monday morning to draw more wood with his uncle's wagon than he broke it—overloaded, I expect. He wanted then to use Father's wagon and caused some coldness there.

"Since I don't have use of Uncle Myron's wagon—" Otis said.

"—Since you broke it, true?" Father challenged.

"It was old, Sir, and just waiting for the day it would collapse—Uncle would say so himself!" Though he used the "Sir," he stiffened up with it.

---

[17] a leavening like baking soda or baking powder, for baked goods

"Perhaps," Father answered, waiting for what his son-in-law would say next. "Well . . . ?"

"I was hoping you would allow me to borrow yours to get to town. I need more things for our place, for Rosette's housekeeping," Otis answered, humbly.

"Where? To Portland?" A Churchill has a mercantile there, where Otis might have more credit.

"No, Sir, just to Lyons, maybe Ionia. I have sugar to sell—almost sixty pounds."

"Well, that will buy a few things, certain," Father nodded. This arrangement needed care from him, as he didn't want Otis to drive our horse too fast or take chances with the wagon, but he didn't want to shame Otis, either. "How would it be if Solomon drove with you? I understand he has business in Ionia—right, Son?"

"Yes, Father, I do."

"And then perhaps next day, Solomon and I can help you with your shanty. My work is in a lull at present."

"Thank you, Sir," Otis answered. "I could do it myself, of course, but extra hands are a help."

And that is how Otis and I came to jog along to town together for more of his home things. The wagon was a sight for the Lyons people after we'd bought his goods in Ionia and amused those citizens with them first—they pointed and laughed at our cantilevered bedstead, rolls of batting, a set of four matching chairs, roll of bedcord, and the things they couldn't see tucked into the wagon. All we two young men needed were a couple of young ladies tied into the back of the wagon with bedcord and we'd have a ready-made double household! Otis was too pleased to care, with his five-dollar bedstead purchase—the nicest they sold—with a curving headboard and smaller matching footboard. Both had arches and vertical posts, with screw-on china newel post tops. Mother and Father have wooden ones, in a leaf design Father carved himself and attached like corks into bottles. We drove back across the river and up the hill, the poor horses pulling hard. But Otis did not urge them harshly.

Next morning we three men, and the boys—who would not be left behind—set out for Otis's home place and helped him almost complete his shanty. When we got back to our home we found Rosette and some ladies at the quilting frame, working on something she called a "brick-work" pattern. Jennette was of the party and spent the night here, and I took her back into the woods and showed her the playhouse. Otis and Rosette did the same less than a year ago, the first days they met—and where are they now? Married and ready to welcome a baby to their home almost built.

I found it easy to talk to Jennette of Otis and Rosette, of their plans, as a way of suggesting the idea of marriage. Of course any young schoolteacher must have in mind that her work might bring her to a husband, but I have not mentioned the idea to her before this. I did not know if she would have it, but I offered to take her to her father's near Grand Rapids the next day, instead of Father. He suggested the thing, to let Mr. and Mrs. Watson see me proper. Though it seems sudden, and I am not ready to propose, I think it is a good idea.

* * *

And so it was. Jennette was all blushes with her family as she introduced me, and they a bit wary, but we got through the stiffness. I conducted myself well at the preaching service, making sure to sing out strong that they might hear my voice and know my piety. Jennette seemed to take some proprietorship of me, seeing me at a disadvantage with her family, and so we have advanced a little in our way together.

We returned home Sunday night to find Otis and Rosette had enough of a shanty to have removed there already, and Jennette will have Rosette's old place at the McKelveys'. Father lent them his wagon and horse to fetch some things stored around all over—at the Kinneys' and Kings' and McKelveys'. Mother loaded me up with bread, butter, cake, pudding, and meat for two or three days, so Rosette does not have to worry about her pantry quite yet. I also took some buttermilk, coffee, salt, and a few other items that will keep longer. I arrived to find no one at home and went across the road to speak to the Longs and their little son. I asked Wellington if he knew his namesake, and he piped off Tennyson's lines:

> With honor, honor, honor, honor to him,
> Eternal honor to his name.

I replied that he needed also to learn the part before:

> And keep the soldier firm, the statesman pure;
> Till in all lands and thro' all human story
> The path of duty be the way to glory.[18]

I expect the little gentleman will know it all very soon, as he tripped off dragging his stick against the pig-fence pilings, calling, "The so-der firm, the stay-sum pure!"

In the shanty I looked around and thought it charming with everything just so and not yet soiled from use. I arranged Mother's gifts on the table and took my leave. In the days to come I will enjoy seeing the husband's care of his home—Otis will make things for Rosette just as she needs them. She will place orders as at a store: a wash

---

[18] Alfred, Lord Tennyson, *Ode on the Death of the Duke of Wellington* (London: Edward Moxton, 1852). https://books.google.com

bench to put the new tub and board upon, a cupboard for the plates we bought last week, a vessel for soap.

Otis and I went to Father's one late morning and left Rosette to see to her housekeeping. I expect she was glad not to have the dinner and supper preparations for us. She could get on with her arrangements—one thing upon another, not all at once. Otis still has the house things to make and brought along a narrow post that he had turned on the lathe and was whittling down on the ends as we walked. I soon found it was becoming a decorated rolling pin. He does such fine work. I remarked as much to Rosette later, and she showed me her palms and said his mop-stick left her no splinters, and was smooth as smooth. I called that day just in time to have some of her first bread worked on Otis's bread board, baked in their stove, and it was pretty fine—I was surprised! Otis was away getting a pail of soap of his Aunt Lucinda, until Rosette makes her own—another job she has never done. She said she would borrow flatirons of Mrs. Long until Otis could get her some of her own.

I came back two days later, in unseasonable chill and blustery rain, to bring some little thing from Mother and to find Otis had been transplanting cabbages—seventy plants—and chopping all manner of firewood. At least it is his own now, and not just his contribution to a household that is keeping him or his bride. Wellington must have spied me coming and soon was over with some green currants from his mother to Rosette, who told him to tell his mother she was an excellent neighbor. "Yes, ma'am!" he agreed and ran out again, but not before crossing the room to my chair and laying a proprietary hand upon my knee without a word.

Not long after, he came in again with some lettuce and vinegar. Rosette sent the vinegar back, saying, "Wellington, please thank your mother for me, but I have my own vinegar from Mr. Churchill's sugar-bush—so much that I have no place to keep any more of it!" We enjoyed lettuce dressed with her vinegar, and she saved some for Otis's late supper in case he came. She showed me how she heads her journal pages now with "Orange," our township home.

Even though it was late when I left, I went back home again by bright moonlight, with contented thoughts of the Churchills' new home.

Father took my place next day to see about the new householders. Mother wrapped up Dutch cheese and cake to send and when he came back she pressed for details. He said Clarinda met him along the way with flowers, for Rosette. And when he arrived Mrs. Long had just taken over a pound of butter, so everyone is supplying them well. They see Rosette growing bigger and bigger with child and want to ease her way.

I missed a few days seeing their place filling out as a home, but Jennette went to visit and brought me a report. She took off her bonnet as she stepped into the barn, then swept back a tendril of her golden hair and told off the points on the fingers of one hand, as if she rehearsed them on the walk over. Her voice filled my heart and it was all I could do not to grasp those fingers in mine.

When Jennette arrived Otis was abed, trying to stop a nosebleed that had not abated all the afternoon. Myron King must have repaired his wagon, she said, for Otis used it to get griddles for the stove, and a lifter and rim. Rosette proudly showed her each item. The ladies went outside to enjoy a bit of sunshine after the rain, but the mosquitoes soon chased them in again.

Next day Otis was here to supper and visited a while, saying he'd finished hoeing his potatoes and chopped more trees—so many pleasant hours of light this time of year. Next day, Jennette told me, Rosette was at the McKelveys' getting a basin of lard Ann promised her. Jennette welcomed her to join school with her and her pupils, knowing she was missing it. Jennette would make Rosette a fine sister.

From the Journal of
Rosette Churchill
July 1857

    Wednesday 29th. Otis cradled for Uncle M. again. Mrs. Long ate dinner with me & brought me some string beans. Two showers P.M.
    Thursday 30th. Very warm. I went to fathers & boiled the soap. It is quite good.

Sally - First Fruits

ROSETTE IS GETTING ON SO WELL with her housekeeping! I took a walk to her new home, carrying some new milk and dried apples with a few other little things, and showed her how to soak the apples for a skillet cake. Otis would be hungry when he came home from hoeing Mr. King's corn. "Mother, look at these enormous gooseberries Otis brought me the other day!" she exclaimed, holding them out.

"They are as big as cherries," I agreed. "Do you remember a painting we saw in New York—with gooseberries in a bowl, on a white cloth?"

"No, I do not recall it," she said.

"Well, you were small back then."

She had Otis pin up her Michigan map in their shanty, and it looks well at the end of the room, above the table. Rosette pinned a scarlet thread along their honeymoon journey route, and I asked her to show me the places they had stopped, and to tell me more about Otis's relations.

"Mother, I never told you about the evening at Uncle Henry Garter's, when he played his fiddle to this song . . ." She leaned over to the shelf and took out her journal, turning to the place. "Nelly was a lady," she sang after the verse. "Last night she died. Toll the bell for lubly Nell, my dark Virginny bride."

"So sad, like the old ballads."

"It's Stephen Foster, who has many lovely songs," she replied. "It makes me wonder how the slaveholders could continue to hold slaves, thinking that they could fall in love, and marry and be bereaved, like the rest of us."

"Somehow they do, though," I said.

"I once saw a free couple—that had been slaves. They were at a house near Ionia."

"Yes, I've heard of them."

"And they were neat and clean and seemed as pleasant as anyone." She closed her journal and set it on the shelf again.

It is well I picked that day to walk over, for the next was cold enough for a fire burning all day, and the next, as well. I sent Jacob over, he thinking it was his idea, to offer Otis the red cow for thirty dollars, and to wait a year for his pay. Fresh milk would be so good for mother and babe in the year to come, but I do not know whether Otis will take it. He just received settlement from Mr. McKelvey for the ox he killed with his felled tree. (We had no help for the spilled syrup a few days later—Jacob would not press for it.) I think they are settling well with funds for their future.

Otis came here for sugar and buttermilk one morning and stayed for dinner with us. Knowing he likes to arrange things for himself, I asked, "How should we prepare for when the baby arrives?"

"Well," he said, "I've thought of that. Babies don't usually come quickly, as I understand."

"Not the first," I answered, "Though it is well to be prepared for whatever might occur."

"I could come here in early hours to send you over to Rosette, and I would then go on to fetch the doctor."

"Yes, and I can help Rosette prepare all the things we will need," I agreed. "I'll get a woman or two to go with me, whoever is handy." We quieted as if to say it was all settled, but I added, "You do well to get her milk and berries and things as she has a taste for them. Ramsdells have always been a strong lot, and I credit the variety of our food." The women in these parts will continue to supply for them in the next few months. Each babe is a blessed new hope for us all, though we will lose some, and mothers, too.

The next day Otis was to work on the road, and I cautioned him to be sure someone checked on Rosette when he must be away for a full day or long evening. I am indeed glad that Mrs. Long is just across the road from them.

While Otis was working, then, I set out to visit, carrying another bunch of Clarinda's flowers. She likes to share them, especially as she thinks of the dark in that shanty, she told me, before the window goes in. Along the way I stopped at Mr. McKelvey's and picked up Ann and Jennette and we made a happy party to see Rosette in her little home. We gave her counsel on her crust, as Mrs. Kinney had brought her pie-plant[19] the day before. Jennette gently took the knife from Rosette and began crunching through the stalks as she talked her into a chair, then hooked a foot to slide up a box for her feet. All at once Rosette was at rest and Jennette at her work. We hardly saw it happen.

---

[19] a term for rhubarb

Next day Otis was at our place again, and I sent him back with Rosette's new *Journal of Education*. She saw the writers of this journal when they spoke at the Institute last September, likely her last event of that sort. She would not have known then that she would be here now, great with child, in her new home, with a husband she had never laid eyes on at that date. It is funny to think of it. I asked Ellen to take Frank and some of the others after their lessons to see Rosette, and they made a children's parade of it. I am glad to have this daughter growing into a woman beside me now that Rosette is gone for good. One woman cannot do all for a household of this size!

When Otis came to chop here I urged him, "Do bring Rosette tomorrow, that she might work in the light, and get away from your little place for a bit." He looked at me disapprovingly and I realized what I'd said, so I cast about for some way to praise something about the place—"Ah, what a clever broom! Did you make this?"

"Yes," he answered. "From a branch, until I can get another at Ionia."

I hope that was not the wrong thing to mention. I must take care he knows I am happy with his husbanding. Jacob watches closely and forms his own opinions without saying a word.

When Rosette was with me she fairly bubbled over all the gifts the ladies have made to her—of course Clarinda's flowers and lettuces, Mrs. Allen's onions, and Mrs. King's eggs and my cake. I did not think of eggs—I don't know why—but I hope Otis will get some hens and a rooster for Rosette soon. Perhaps I can mention it to him, if I am careful. He told Jacob he did not want the cow after all, and he was stiffly courteous about that. I will see what I can do to supply some of the milk they will miss. Clarinda thought also of tomato plants and a pan of moss to keep out mosquitoes now, and to stop the chinks in the walls for winter.

I have been helping Rosette learn how to make her own soap at our place, with rain-barrel water put up over the top of the ash-leach. But she does not have lye enough yet and I will put this in the kettle with the grease and let it stand until she gets more ashes. It is dirty work but she is getting it and feels rightly proud. The difficult part is yet to come, and we will see how that goes. Jennette came and kept company with us, and both stayed until after supper, then walked back to their places in our long summer evening. When next I saw Rosette at her home she read from her journal:

> *The sky at twilight was covered with clouds formed into all imaginable different and beautiful shapes, & the lightning flashed almost incessantly from every point of the compass except the north.*

She writes better than she knows.

I sent Jacob to see Rosette a day or two later, and he met her on her way to the Kinneys' and said she was going to the Kings' after that, and the school. I suppose she is feeling well to be so much about. When Otis came here the day following, he said Kinneys were eating new potatoes already, having planted a bit before we and he had planted. I do look forward to those. Rosette later told me Ann brought beets for greens to her, and Mr. McKelvey—Colonel—gave her some green apples. A bit of the harvest is coming to us now, and the wheat is readying.

With a new provision of ashes, Rosette was able to continue with her soap and did fairly well with it while Otis was off to Lyons with Myron King. But Otis inspected the soap and said, "Rosette, you must boil this more." She did not reply. I am glad I did not say anything myself, but then I hadn't even seen it, being taken up with my own work.

Otis, when he is not testing soap for quality, is cradling wheat for Mr. King, and then for himself. He sold his steer to a butcher for three dollars—a small sum for such a good one, I told Rosette confidentially—and took fifteen dollars' savings and put it toward the stove debt. "That was a sensible thing to do," I told her when she came here to split some straw and have some of my raspberry sauce.

"Jerome! Frank!" I called when she was ready to leave. "Walk your sister back home as far as the corners. Now that Jennette is here, we have work to get on with." The school teacher kept me womanly company for the afternoon. She is a lively golden thing to Rosette's somber rose. Rosette can be girlish and have fun, but she seems almost to have to insist that she is having a lark when others would just enjoy it. For Jennette, joy springs up from her to refresh all those around, and she considers each one's need. She makes good company for all of us, even as much as we differ among ourselves. I am glad Solomon is setting his sights on her.

From the Journal of
Rosette Churchill
August 1857

Wednesday 5th. Pleasant & cool. Otis went to Uncle M's again to cradle. I finished a hat for Mr. Barber.

Friday 7th. I went to father's & staid all day & cut two striped shirts for Otis & partly made one. Elsie came up to see me after supper & she [and] Ellen came with me as far as the corners when I came home, & soon after Otis overtook me.

Rosette - Queen

I AM A BALL FIT TO BURST, stiller every day with the heat, just waiting. I used to be so quick in my school, or at dancing, and now I stay where I put myself, the effort to rise too burdensome. At least when I can stay down I do. But so much must be done. I am furiously sewing, making my way through that factory cloth Otis bought for me not long back. So many keep me company as I work, and bring me things to ease my housekeeping until we have all our own stores.

The first day of the month I had no sooner come back from breakfasting at Mr. Long's, bearing currants Mrs. Long sent with me, than Frank came on his own. The little mite brought a sack of onions from Mama and Mrs. Barber. He kept me company a couple of hours, then scampered back home, proud of his independence, and came back after dinner with Jerome for the afternoon.

We are surrounded by wheat Otis has been cradling, but the thrashing has not yet begun. Our wheat was not yet ready, giving him time to work for others. Despite the bounty all around us we have no flour of our own, that being the work to come of thrashing and taking it to the mill. So Otis has gotten more flour from Father and his Uncle Myron and hardly had time for that, now needing to cradle his own fast-ripening wheat.

Mrs. Long sent me a mess of peas one rainy day, and I boiled them up with our new potatoes for dinner, with butter. Some days I disappear into my work—I stood in a trance over that pot, watching the half-boiled potatoes bob around with the peas cascading in. I could almost have been Mother a few summers ago, round with Baby Frank and tending her own pot of potatoes and peas.

Until we have our own cow at home I am glad for those who think to give us things. Otis holds back from buying much—he wants us supplying ourselves. And if we owned a cow, I do not know what I would do. I have no need of yet another job to milk it, and all bent over, too. Am I so creaky already at twenty-seven? At least I am doing well with my hand-work and finished a hat for Mr. Barber the pleasant, cool day Otis cradled again for Uncle Myron.

The more he is at his work and I at my own, the better things are. When we are at work here together, or when his work day is done, the little storm clouds gather. He sees me fumble at the cooking, or scowls if he finds me abed easing my back or shading my eyes from a headache. To be fair, he does not push me more than he does himself, but I can find no rest when he is about. Sometimes he whips up into such a tempest that it is best if he can get off to town for a half-day or overnight. He comes back with things for our home, and I delight in those and he in my delight. But it does not last long.

One hot, still dawn I was awake before Otis. Using the chamber pot as I needs must so often these days, I carried it out with me to empty it, then tucked up my nightdress to sit on the doorstep, quieting myself for the day to come. The sun heated my hair on one side and I shaded my eyes from it. I listened to the chirruping and whirring of wings as the birds flew about me—some had made a nest already under our new roof, but the fledglings were grown and flown, and the nest had fallen to the ground. All was early, and lively, and young, in that quiet moment of July.

But then a shove and a thump and grumbled curse inside clutched my heart like a fist. I cast my eyes up to review with dismay what must have gotten in his way, and what my part was in that. What had I done? A chair scraped and banged, and I scurried in to start breakfast. Father never betrayed such temper as an ongoing current just below the good manners, and I do not know how best to respond.

The days are much the same for me—I sit here in the shanty or just outside in good weather, plying my needle and waiting for whatever visitor Providence is sending me that day. I sat at Mrs. Long's all one afternoon finishing a shirt, after she'd sent me a cucumber for dinner by way of invitation. Late afternoon, after their supper, Mother and Clarinda appeared, completely loaded down with eatables and flowers. I set them aside, ate supper with Mrs. Long, and then carried home the bounty—pancakes already buttered, lettuce, onions, goose-berry pie, and flowers. From Clarinda an apple pie, more onions, peas, more flowers, a carrot, two cucumbers and two large beets. Aunt Lucinda hailed Clarinda on the way to bring those from her, and Clarinda met Mother at the corners. Little Wellington helped me carry the things home—what would I do with all of it?

Next day I wanted a walk, the temperature being cool and pleasant. I went to cut and sew a bit at Mother's, then Ellen and Elsie saw me to the corners, and from there Otis overtook me. I am scarcely out of anyone's sight these days. All are watching and waiting.

On our way back home that night, I asked Otis what plans he had beyond the harvest, and whether he was happy with our life as it is now. I peered at his face. He furrowed his brow and looked straight ahead. "I am content. You are learning your house-ways, all of them," he said deliberately. "Though you do not have the strength sometimes of a farm woman, you make an effort. And your sewing provides."

I squeezed his arm in appreciation. "I hope once the baby is here, I will be able to do more of the hard work."

"And I, too, Rosette," he answered. "We must keep in good economy, but I want you to look well, and to be a credit to me."

"I do hope to be that, Otis," I said quietly. My words hung in the air. He wrapped his arm about my shoulders.

* * *

I was glad to get opportunity to finish a lawn cape for Aunt Lucinda one morning. Ellen brought me the alternating bands of cloth—one sheer, one plain, one lace. It was a pleasure to work with the stuff. All the children came to fetch it in the afternoon. I added the two shirts I made for Henry, with my little maple leaf on the button placket. I make it very small, in thread to match the cloth, so it is more felt than seen. But it is my mark. After a fitful night with little sleep I suffered the colic for an hour or so. Otis must have told them at home, for Father called to see about me. I was glad to show myself peaceful and resting with the last pages of *Legends of the West*.

Otis, between his jobs with all the harvests, made a trip to Lyons and brought me back a beautiful pair of calfskin shoes. My ankles are mostly still trim and well formed, and the new shoes laced up smoothly, though I can scarcely see them! He made me go to Ann's next day when he could not watch with me. Jennette brightened the place when she came to stay all night herself. Solomon is blessed in her, and has told me he means to ask her father by letter for her hand, so he can ask her while she is still here, before he takes her home at the end of the school term. She is another of his sort, walking free and easy in the world, sure of the Almighty's favor. She speaks of the Savior with sweet affection, as if He were another man like Solomon, or Father. I do not know how I can be all dark strivings and Solomon bright ease. Jennette can sit with her hands loose in her lap when not working, while mine are always in motion, turning some object round and round, or even scratching with some phantom pen, writing words on the air.

Otis came for me when his work was done, bringing ripe whortleberries from Mrs. Kinney. Visitors came while I was away, for cake and flowers lay on the table, and I added Ann's cucumbers to the harvest, as I call it—a harvest of visiting. The next day Mrs. Long brought her work here and quietly watched without seeming to. I hope to keep this babe inside as long as possible, though it is so wearying to my days. A different kind of weariness will follow when it is here among us. And meantime we put all in readiness.

With his team, Uncle Myron helped Otis draw his wheat and stack it at Father's—five loads! I was glad to give him dinner in our little place, though it was with his own wife's provisions—since she sent me some squashes and cucumbers. Just at nightfall some cousins I have not seen for a while stopped by to see our place. Nancy Dunsmore and I stepped out for a pail of water, and she giggled to show me her bloomers like mine. She looked as neat as a doll in them.

"Please go back with us to your father's," Nancy cried, grasping my hand as we stepped back into the shanty.

I could not imagine making the walk after a weary day, and said, "No, I cannot manage it tonight, but perhaps Otis could go with you—"

"No," he said. "If you cannot, I WILL not." I smiled at him. When they left we spent a quiet evening together—some days are pleasant like that.

It is funny to think of grown men gathering berries as little children do, but since the whortleberries require wading through the swamp, Uncle Myron and Colonel McKelvey and Otis were to make an expedition of it for us. But then, as the rain increased, they thought better of it. The cold blustering lasted all day. A misty day followed, and Otis kept under the lean-to at our place and made shingles.

The day Ann sent me the first green corn and Otis brought almost a pound of butter from Uncle Myron's, I made a treat of corn pudding for Otis and whoever else might call at dinnertime that day. I borrowed a little milk of the Longs and of course used our sugar, and we had a feast. No one else came by, though, so we ate it again for supper and were content. The next day Ann sent some sceotash[20] along, so we were beginning to be a little weary of corn.

Amos Utter and Charles Coon with his machine were at Father's for the thrashing, and it was quite the enterprise. Otis told me how it was all done in two days, and now he has seventy-four bushels of his own. Saturday Father lent his oxen for Otis to draw it home to his bin he made for the harvest. How satisfied he is, even whistling a little as he set out "a-whortleberrying," as he called it, this morning. He came back with six quarts, having picked up Colonel McKelvey along the way, and bringing from Ann more butter, squashes, and cucumbers. Mother came to supper, but mostly brought her own, with sweet milk, gooseberries, onions, and green corn. She whisked up a skillet corn pudding for us without sugar, but with her

---

[20] a variation on the spelling of "succotash"

good onions and lots of pepper. It was a chilly day, so the warm stuff was good for supper.

The thrashing machines have moved to Uncle Myron's and of course Otis was there to help. Mrs. Long and Mrs. Howe called on me together, Mrs. Long to borrow some flour. But I know they wanted to check in on me, then went back to have their supper together at the Longs'. Wellington showed up the next afternoon to return the borrowed flour, and more, of course, and was happy to be made a fuss of by my visitors that day, Cousin Almona, aunts, and Ann.

When Otis brought the rest of my dresser from Father's, our house felt finished in its preparations for our child. I got some work done and sent—including Mr. Barber's other hat. And what did I see as I sent Otis out but Amos Utter with his cow, which he claimed not to want to drive home just then.

"Mrs. Churchill, this cow has been no end of bother for me the last days, and I am ready to be shut of her for a while. Do you think I could tie her here for a day or two?"

"Well, of course, Mr. Utter," I answered. "I am sure Mr. Churchill would be happy to do you that favor. If you want to tie her to that tree over there, where she has some grass in the clearing, my husband can confine her under the lean-to for the night."

"I would be much obliged, then," he said, as he squared his hat back on his head and led the cow to the tree I indicated. "Do you think," he called over his shoulder, "that I could borrow a pail and a little stool of you so I can milk her? May I leave the milk with you in payment?"

"Well, of course, Mr. Utter," I said, seeing his intent. So here we are with a borrowed cow for a few days. How good these people are to me!

From the Journal of
Rosette Churchill
September 1857

Saturday 5th. Ellen came home with me after breakfast. I had the cholic all A.M. & was sick again at evening. Otis went for Mrs. Long & mother who came.

Sunday 6th. Cold. Otis got Mrs. Kinney about 1 in the morning & sent for Dr. Gilbert, who got here about 4 hours later. And we had a little son who came into this world about 3 o'clock in the morning & who weighs 6 ¾ lbs. Aunt Lucinda, & Sarah Maria, Ann, Mrs. Williams, Mrs. Phinesey & Mrs. Kinney called P.M. & father, Jerome & Frank in the morning.

Monday 7th. Mother came in the morning & worked some. Mrs. Howe called at night. Father called & Old Dr. Lanbourn with him.

Wednesday 16th. Rainy. I dressed myself for the first time since my sickness.

Sally - Convalescence

T WAS OTIS AND ROSETTE'S eight-month anniversary that first day of September, and we would have at least an eight-months babe, for which I was thankful, though Rosette's time seemed likely to come any day. Otis was to be at home working nearby the first day or two, and then I hoped to take her home in the wagon with me for a while.

On the fourth, a Friday, I got her home to our place and settled her with Mrs. Howe and her mother to quilt all day. She seemed peaceful and comfortable, and I persuaded her to spend the night with us. In the morning she would go back, and Ellen went with her. I watched them out of sight making their slow way. Ellen came back by dinnertime, saying Rosette was gripped by the colic all morning, then slept a little before she left her to come home, Otis working just outside in case of need. And as I expected, before supper Otis was in the yard.

"Mother Ramsdell," he called through the kitchen window as he came to the back door, "I think it is time that Rosette have you with her."

"You didn't leave her alone, did you?" I quickly pulled out a cold supper the men could have while I was away.

"No, I got Mrs. Long first, and told Wellington to run after me if there was need."

"Good," I said. "Then let me get some things and come with you."

"I am going on to tell Dr. Gilbert—"

"Likely he won't be needed for many hours," I warned.

"But I would have him know in any case, to be at the ready," Otis explained. "You will be all right to go on your own? If you leave your bag here, I will pick it up on my way back."

"That would be kind of you, Otis. Thank you."

My mind was racing, and of course I needed to gather some foodstuffs to take along, and peppermint tea in case she wanted some—another thing they must still plant. Time enough for that in the next spring. After packing the bags Otis would carry, I took one myself and asked Frank if he wanted to come with me.

"To see a baby?" he asked.

"Not yet, but soon, I think. You may have to stay out in the yard, but I expect Wellington will be in need of company. Here, carry this with you—two maple wax candies for you to share."

"Oh, good!" he exclaimed, stuffing the little bundle into his pocket and choosing a walking stick for himself from the collection on the porch. He got me one, too. I am not yet old, but I confess I enjoy having a stick when I can, to save my strength.

When we turned off the road toward their shanty I could see Wellington Long squatting at the door, dragging a bunch of wheat straw through the dirt. Frank leaped ahead and ran right up to him, paused a moment, then darted around the corner, on the way to the stream, no doubt. Wellington brightened up and ran after him. No use telling them to be careful—boys never will. At least they were out of the way for a while.

Inside, Mrs. Long made way for me as I entered, saying Rosette had slept some and was resting quietly, her pains coming only every once in a while. She made her excuses and slipped away to her place—I heard her call the boys over for supper. There I was with my eldest—one of two remaining daughters. I was about to become a grandmother.

The both of us would be transformed in the coming night, passed over from one time of life to another. All would become for her Before and After. Marriage did not make that change for me as much as did motherhood, since my soul was bound to Jacob's in my mind long before we wed. But no imagination can call up the way the whole world colors differently when a new babe—a first one—lies in our arms. We think we know how it will be, watching our mothers and sisters, changing the soiled linen, bouncing a wailing mite just so to calm him, but we do not know. Not yet.

Rosette has taken her time of expecting as a matter of course, the next in a series of tasks to take on. A little sooner than expected—perhaps, perhaps not—but it will not matter now, as all is decently arranged, and thankful I am for that! I will not intrude to tell her all she must learn on her own—we do not get on well together with much of that. I answer questions as she has them, though I expect she saves the closer ones for Mrs. Long, or Ann McKelvey. Rosette and I have always had different concerns, and here, too, we are finding our way, more formal than some. She is often silly but just as often iron-strong with her determination. I am glad she has let me indulge her a little with the cakes and flowers and things of late, and I will continue that for a while to come—my first daughter, my first grandchild.

* * *

And so in the course of the hours Rosette drew closer to her time of delivery. The colic increased and grew more regular, not giving her rest. It made this stalwart daughter give a little, as when a headache or toothache takes her to bed. She gave herself into my care and let me bathe her brow and help her into a new nightdress when hers became too damp for comfort. I suffered her to walk the few paces around the bed with my arm for support, and she knelt on the bed and grasped one of the china-topped posts, curving around it to ease her back. I made Otis stay outside, handing him some bread and cheese through the door when supper-time was long past. I was glad when Mrs. Long appeared at the door again and I could have her make the peppermint tea for Rosette to sip, and for us, too. She told me quietly that Frank trotted home after supper when he learned no baby had yet appeared.

Finally after midnight it seemed we were drawing much closer. I directed Otis to send for the doctor. Otis went to fetch Mrs. Kinney to help me, then ran to the doctor's, beyond our place. He got back just before his son came into the world, about three o'clock by Rosette's watch. The doctor did not come for four hours after Otis fetched him, but the baby came in two! Mrs. Kinney and I got yet another nightdress for Rosette—one I brought. We washed her face and limbs and arranged her linen, then tucked her up pretty in the bed with the babe. We called Otis to see his little family, and he came in with a bit of straw in his hair from where he had dozed in the shed. We ladies bundled up the wash for later and made Rosette and Otis breakfast—and ourselves, too.

We were having a little party in the candlelight, still dark before dawn, when Doctor Gilbert arrived, pleased to see everything had gone well, and apologizing for his delay. We scarcely heard what kept him, and he was gone again in a trice.[21] At dawn Mrs. Kinney stepped over to the Longs' to find a bit of a place to lay her head, and I bent my own over the table, finding the hard wooden chair as soft as I required. Otis pulled his chair up by the bed and rested against the bedpost, laying one hand across his swaddled baby and over Rosette's arm that held the bundle. They made quite a pretty picture.

We all slept an hour or two, then the day began. Otis gently pulled his arm away from his wife and baby, washed his face in the bowl in the corner, and fetched new water for me. I stretched up from my place, found my bags that Otis brought me last night, and pulled out a cake and a fresh apron and began another breakfast. Rosette stirred after that, the babe still asleep. I helped her change the cloths again and then woke her son to suckle.

In the growing daylight I could hear Otis about his morning chores. I helped my daughter with the first of hers as a new mother, showing her how to look to the needs of her child. Babies are fragile, the wonder of their arrival always with a shadow over it, the shadow of uncertainty. We all know this, and smile tenderly, almost afraid to hope, quiet in reverence and fear. Jacob wouldn't like it, but I wish Cousin Betsy were here to tell the baby's fortune or call upon Diana beyond to see what will be with this one. This young fellow is hearty—Otis used a hanging scale to weigh him at six and three-quarter pounds. He has good color, pale hair swirled above his ruddy brow.

The quiet morning gave way to all manner of visitors. First came Jacob with Jerome and Frank, who would climb up on the bed against all remonstrance, as Rosette said. Frank, being the youngest around here, is ready to have someone to lord it over, and Jerome is quite proud to be an uncle now. Jacob winked at me from the doorway when

---

[21] "in a trice" – quickly

he asked if Grandpa might come in. Otis beams behind his stiffness with all the visitors—several ladies in the afternoon with Ellen, all bearing food, a couple of them willing to look around for some work that needed doing. That evening, I went home with Jacob and the boys, taking the bundle of wash, sure Rosette would be fine kept to bed, and knowing Mrs. Long would help see to that. As I gathered my things, Rosette asked me to give her her pen and bottle and her journal, which I was glad to do. A special day to get down in those pages!

Next morning I walked back to do for the young family and found Otis beginning some of Rosette's chores. I told him I plan to come as much as I can—though I didn't suggest he call a girl in for that purpose. He knows what he can afford. Jacob came again and brought old Dr. Lanbourn with him, who must pronounce on the fitness of the child though he cannot be bothered to come out for a delivery anymore. It was a ceremony, and Jacob is one for the Event when it seems right to him.

I did go back the next two days, and among us Mrs. Long, Otis, and I did all of Rosette's work as well as our own. Otis said he tried to get one of the Howe girls to come but was not successful, though the young girls come to visit regularly enough. They want to play and then scamper away, not come in for the cooking and washing. Ah, well, their time will come, and I do not mind it. Four days after the delivery Otis was able to get one of the Sutton girls, Mary Jane, so I came to help direct her in how things should be done. She did fairly well, but when I arrived the next afternoon all was in arrears.

Rosette lay pale on the pillow, and when I checked, her linens were sorely in need of changing. Otis had seen me from the field, I suppose, and came in just after that.

"What happened, Otis? Where is Mary Jane?" I asked, finding the baby's linen soiled, as well.

"It seems she got homesick, and I am not sure what to do here," he answered. "I do not make very fine a housekeeper, nor nursemaid."

"Well, I will do what I can," I said. "At least I can make you both a supper and take the laundry back with me. Or you can bring it yourself—it is quite the bundle."

"I have told both King and McKelvey I would cut corn for them, and that work is waiting for tomorrow," he said, ending on an uncertain note.

"Then," I said finally, "there is no help for it, and I will come back in the morning. These two seem to be faring pretty well, as well as we can expect."

"Thank you," he said, and meant it. I could see relief allow his shoulders to bend in fatigue.

Ten days past the birth, Rosette was up and about and dressed, more like herself, though I cautioned her to go easy with things and kept myself around to see to that. Otis came in that afternoon with some apples from Myron King's and five pounds of butter, ten shillings'[22] worth, from Ann McKelvey. I directed him to go to our place to borrow a sieve and a box for it.

When he was gone, Rosette took down her journal and wrote a few lines at the table, then blew across the ink. The baby slumbered on the bed, then stirred, clenching his little fist above his head and grimacing as he arched his back. We laughed a little, at the precious familiar actions of an infant.

"Mother—Mama," she said, to start a question. "How should I think about my babe? I delight in his little body and the way he moves his mouth and opens his eyes, and I feel the milk stir in me when he calls."

"That is all as it should be," I answered.

---

[22] a unit of currency still in use in 1850s America, worth 24 or 25 cents

"But I do not feel stirrings of love for him as I thought I would." She brushed the feather of her pen across the dry side of the page, then drew her finger along the edge of the feather, joining the divided parts and twirling the pen in her fingers. "I care for him, and would do all he needs, but my heart does not call to him."

"Perhaps," I said, "you will feel those stirrings more as he grows. When he can look at you a-purpose and crawl to you—"

"—And talk to me! Perhaps that is all I need, just to have him older, like one of my pupils." He stirred on the bed again and she rose from the table to fetch him, to feel for dampness in his cloths. She pursed her lips against his temple and turned his downy head against her cheek. They look well, in any case, in the sunshine streaming through the door.

* * *

I believe Otis has now settled with McKelvey on the ox incident, and we had a first frost. The next day I was not happy to see Rosette with the colic again—that should all be past now. I stayed with her while Otis cut buckwheat at our place for Jacob, after corn at the McKelveys'. Our millet is well in now, thanks in part to Otis. I have weaned away from their shanty a little at a time, though I sent a dressed chicken in my place yesterday. But perhaps it was too soon. Rosette invited all the children to supper (I made sure they took the supper, so as not to give her more work), and when they returned they said that she was in the colic again, and Otis away at the fair.

Hearing Otis banging on the kitchen door long before dawn I felt my heart give way. It seems he had come home in the middle of the night and found Rosette ill, with Mrs. Long and Mrs. Kinney there, but none knew what to do for her. I listened to what he told me and gathered my things to doctor her. He hitched up the wagon, at Jacob's insistence and with his help, and we hastened along the road in the balmy darkness.

Once there I gave Rosette suppositories and wrapped her warmly, then soaked her feet as the dawn caught up with us. She thrashed and groaned for hours. Finally about eleven o'clock she vomited and later said how relieved she was at having got rid of "the dreadful load," the worst she'd ever known. We laughed at that, cleaned her up, and began to be a little easy.

Rosette soon recovered, and the baby suckles so much that the mother is quite hungry. Her eyes grew large at the peaches Otis brought in for her, and I gave her some cheese. She is better.

Otis is about ready to log again, and gathering seed cucumbers and squashes for next year's planting. Already it is time. Jennette and Maria came to supper and Rosette announced to all of us that they will call the baby DeWitt,[23] after our New York Governor as was. She is well enough that she went across to Mrs. Long's and got some buttermilk. I think they are settled now and we can all begin full preparations for winter.

---

[23] spelled "DeWit" throughout the journal, but "DeWitt" in later legal documents and on his gravestone

*From the Journal of
Rosette Churchill
October 1857*

Sunday 4th. I am holding DeWit (as I generally do now-a-days when I write) or he wiggles about so, I make bad work.

Wednesday 7th. Warm. Uncle M. & Mr. Mc. K. logged for Otis & boarded themselves.

Thursday 8th. Otis commenced digging his potatoes. Warm days & cool nights.

Otis - Adjustment

WE ARE CUTTING CORN NOW, and I'm content to be of use to Long for his, and doing some work for his wife as well. We will make good neighbors.

Rosette is faring decently with our son, though I don't see how she will continue to attend to her close needlework and her journal, as he is already squirming about to jostle her hand. Our son fared well, at first, sleeping and suckling in the usual way, and without much crying in early days, though I can sleep through it in any case. I made him a cradle, but Mother Ramsdell would not let me begin until we named him, saying it was bad luck. She surprises me sometimes with her fears, when other times she works from knowledge and has fancy ways about the house. If I can humor her in that, it gains me elsewhere. So the cradle came later than I wanted.

Now when the women come visiting they have baby things to bring and talk about—butter oil from one and skunk's oil from another. I hardly listen as Rosette tells why one favors one and one the other for the rash. I have potatoes to dig and corn to cut. Traded some wheat with Sol and began my ploughing under for the winter. Some are bringing us apples now, and tame grapes—our plum and cherry trees promise a return in years to come. Then DeWitt can toddle along to help me, and Rosette can tend to another babe or two we will raise up on this place. I do not mind having that Wellington boy about in the meantime, and his folks seem happy enough to leave him in our care. They went off the other day and he came to have supper and a sleep with us when they did not return early enough.

Amos Kinney was here to tell me about the bear he treed but did not kill. I would have liked to see that, though I don't relish having one near here with my family. I will get a dog soon. When I got in from finishing an acre of wheat the other day, and the last of my potatoes, Rosette looked up from the table. Her sister Ellen and her brothers were starting dinner without me and she said, "Look, Otis—Frank has brought DeWitt his rug and boy!" She held out a grimy scrap of knitting and a stiff wooden doll. "The baby has presents before he knows anything about it!" Frank kept his head down, but his ears burned red.

Next day I told Rosette of my mother's way of doing the soap, to see if she can improve, and I did it for her at her folks' place. I also repaired a saw and a bushel basket, and considered how best to tighten us up for winter. On those frost nights I can feel just where the cold creeps in here and on blustery nights blows in there. Brother Sylvester has written me again, saying Mother is well and all continues as before—Henry George still odd, and wandering off some days. We had hoped he would grow out of it. Sylvester sent me another *True Flag*. Rosette likes that, though I haven't much time for it.

I wish I had all my own things, as I am forced to borrow Uncle Myron's wagon and Father Ramsdell's oxen for my lumber. I drawed two loads from Keefer's mill. Father R. offered to sell me his red cow a while back, but I can do without that for now. Until I can buy a cow outright, I will buy a little milk here and there, or Mother Ramsdell will send some with the boys when they come. We saw our first snow—with hail and rain and all—on the nineteenth. I drove the oxen through it with another load of lumber. Then I used the team to draw our soap home— four pails full.

I can work in Rosette's jobs with my own for now, but instead of getting stronger she is weakening. She was querulous with the colic the other evening and now keeps making me look at something coming up at the end of her spine. I don't want all this talk of pimples and welts and baby's rashes. I hate the stink of the baby's cloths hanging about inside when it's wet out. I want to finish our house done as soon as I can, to give us more room and things not so close. The baby has been crying more—and louder—as he's grown, and Rosette does not manage well. I am working in the clearing for our house every spare hour.

Even while she keeps to the shanty with the baby, Rosette can turn her work toward baskets, as Ann McKelvey taught her to make them. I made my own and got some lumber for that purpose the day Father Ramsdell killed a beef and sold us a hind quarter. I am husking corn for him and brought my own basket home to work on for our crop. So much is going on at Ramsdell's I thought to take Rosette and the baby there for a visit. I carried him and we all stayed a day and a night. It was convenient for the work I'm doing there. The schoolteacher Jennette Watson's brother Daniel is there working, though she's home near Grand Rapids until she marries Solomon in the summer. Before he took her back after the term he proposed, and now she can prepare to come to Orange next year.

When I came back home again, Ellen came along to help with the baby so Rosette could get more work done. DeWitt was still crying as much as ever, setting us all on edge so that work was not finished as it should be. Nevertheless I made some candles for the house and finished my basket. I got away next day to Lyons and sold a load of wheat—six shillings a bushel—and got Rosette two flatirons she needed, candlesticks, cotton flannel, and nails and hammer for my needs. I'd been keeping notes in my pencil-book of what we required, for when we had ready cash, and was satisfied when I could cross them off the list. We have glass now, too, and wicking for more candles.

I can't do my own work very well when the nosebleed comes back, as it did the next day, so I just sat there ridiculous in bed with my head thrown back when Marian and Henry came to visit, bringing apples. A man of the Ionia County Bible Society came, too, bringing us a Bible for the house—I think for the baby, though I don't expect he will be reading soon.

After my day in bed I set the glass window into the wall of the shanty, to let in light when the door must be closed for the winter. Our house will not be done until next summer, but now with the window we have a proper home. Just as I finished a sleet started, and we were both satisfied to be inside watching it slide down the panes. We did not feel the storm ourselves with our stove, our quilts, and an apple pie Rosette made for supper.

From the Journal of
Rosette Churchill
November 1857

 Wednesday 4th. Warmer. . . . Marian gave me an invitation to a pareing bee there in the evening & we went & staid all night. . . . Danced after they got done pareing apples.
 Thursday 5th. Rained all the forenoon & some P.M. We came home about noon. Mr. Howe & Mr. Long called to write with our pen & ink. Very warm for the season.
 Friday 6th. High winds & pleasant. Otis husked corn at fathers.

Rosette - Society

MARIAN HOWE CAME HERE Wednesday morning with Frank and both Ellens to give me an invitation for a paring bee, so I took DeWitt and we stayed all night, Otis preferring to stay at home to see to things—he is trying to find every chink in the shanty before winter to cozy us up, and to do the work while it is still warm.

Almost two dozen were there, including McKelveys, Solomon, and Daniel Watson, though I daresay Sol would have preferred Daniel's sister. When we arrived, we saw their big barn set with trestles and lanterns for the work. The glow through the windows and the people mingling in the yard were so pretty I almost didn't mind the drizzle—a warm one. Inside they had arranged all the apples in boxes and baskets by the tables, and overturned barrels for the ladies to sit on. The men did the paring with newly sharpened knives they'd brought for the purpose, and some were especially adept at palming and quartering the small ones and cutting the larger ones into sixths and eighths. Then the ladies would put heavy needles threaded with stout string through each piece to keep the cut sides from touching more than a little, and as the busy fingers flew, the barn was soon garlanded with the apples for drying. They will take them in the house later to dry with the stove and not freeze out in the barn, and they will have an excellent store.

Next began the jolly time, the trestles and barrels cleared away and the peels swept up in preparation for dancing. Of course Sol brought his fiddle, and another played the fife decently, so with the bones and a harmonica, they made quite the band. Sol brought Ellen, too, who seemed nearly grown as she took her place in the dancing. I can just imagine how she would look in my deep maroon paramatta, her russet curls a contrast to my hair's light brown smoothness. I watched a while but danced only a little myself, with the baby and no husband here, and then DeWitt and I went up to bed. I am just an old married lady now.

The next morning, with the marred apples and cores, the men started the cider. Laughing and capering as if they had drunk some cider already, they made a jolly time with a smoky fire out beyond the barn. I could see them from my upstairs window as I fed DeWitt.

I trudged home through mud and puddles in a light rain and got to our place about noon. Mr. Howe came not long after with Mr. Long to write with our pen and ink. I don't know what they were about, perhaps some promissory note between them. I stepped out to the lean-to while they worked a few minutes. The rain of the day gave way to high winds the next, but pleasant still, the land feeling swept clean, ready for the blanket of snow yet to come.

Still in the glow of the party at the Howes', I was cheerful for two days, one so warm we went without a fire part of the day. Otis and Mr. Long worked on the road some, taking us closer to commerce and society beyond what we have known. On Sunday, Father and Mother, Ellen, Solomon, and Daniel came over to see us after dinner, and that was pleasant, though we sat tight packed in the shanty. The men soon found excuse to tour the farm. Father asked Otis to come husk corn at his place next day and he agreed, and Tuesday Father came here with Otis, drawing thirty bushels. The next day they finished the corn field as a few flakes of snow began to fall.

Father is trusting Otis more with his tools and stock, and gave him his team of oxen to draw wood and house logs. We have finished the last of our beef except the drying part. Otis is going around to all his usual places to work with the men and get his share of the yield, and I am staying at home, since it is difficult to carry the baby around. Jerome and Frank came one day, perfect little gentleman callers.

"Rosette!" Jerome called out. "Sister! We have come to see you!"

"Come in, you two," I answered, opening the door with DeWitt on my hip. "You are just in time for a bit of my corn-bread, with buttermilk and syrup."

"Hurrah!" cried Frank, tumbling all but one of his parcels onto the floor. At least it is wood and not dirt, as some are.

"What have you brought me?" I asked, nodding toward his hands.

"Popcorn!" Frank crowed, pulling at the corners of a kerchief that held the prize.

"And your journal and some papers from the post," added Jerome, arranging them to lie on the table.

How many days did I leave my journal at Father's? I wondered. It would be a chore to get the entries caught up aright.

"Tomorrow we will kill another beef," Jerome added. "And Mama wants to know if you want a portion."

"Yes, tell her we will buy a forequarter. We've just finished the fresh meat from the first, so it is a good time." I cut squares of cornbread from the pan, put it in bowls, poured over a little buttermilk, and then let them spoon on syrup I measured out into a cup.

"So, Frank, what do I hear about a six-year-old coming to your house in two days' time?" I asked.

"I don't know about another six-year-old, but I will be one then. I have a birthday!" he said proudly. "I want it to snow and snow so we can coast at the big hill."

"Did you know I almost went over into the ravine there last winter?" He didn't remember hearing about that, so I told him the story of our coasting party, and how the young men rescued me.

"Was it Otis that rescued you?"

"No, he was away then. It was another young man." Just then DeWitt screeched and I went to him. Both brothers are young enough to be my own boys, I thought then, if I had married as early as Mother did. Just before they started home Jared Long called to borrow a candle, and I saw it was time to light my own.

We now have even more corn, as Otis took Mr. Long's oxen and went to Mr. Howe's and got the ten bushels that were his pay for thrashing there last summer. A couple of days later he took a load of wheat to Lyons, where he got only five shillings a bushel for it, again with Mr. Long's team and Mr. Long himself for company. I am glad they're becoming friends and enjoy talking together, not just working.

I think they brought the cold back with them, for it seems to be here in earnest now.

* * *

Thanksgiving has come and gone with me alone here with DeWitt, since all my family were sick with the influenza. Otis was invited all the same, and he said Mother made a chicken pie for them, put together before she felt too ill herself. I thought the cold was settled in for good, but it was warm again two days later. After a busy Sunday of visits here by Marian King, Otis's grandfather Henry Garter, Uncle Amos, and a couple of others, that night I was taken with the influenza myself.

It passed off quickly, and by morning I was better—no fever—but trembling on my feet. With the returning warmth, flies, bugs, and spiders have come out to plague me, and who should appear to visit today, with all in arrears here, but Grandfather Garter again! He is a glad soul, and likes to dandle DeWitt on his knee, saying they should have their portrait made together when the baby has fattened up a bit more and can sit on his own. We bantered about whether I would allow "the little master" to go to town for such a thing, and he made me merry and easy.

"You do well here, my young matron, keeping house for my grandson. He is such a serious one, at full tilt doing whatever it is he is about." And even as he said this we saw Otis flash past the window, and we laughed together. "I see he is making you a proper house, which you need for all the visitors you are having, myself included. But this little hole is pleasant—you have made it so."

That man cheers me. While we were visiting we found more cause to laugh, as Father's pig herd came by, and one rogue scrambled against the fence and pulled it down, so all of them came in. But by running about and with the help of Mr. Long, Otis got it, and asked Father if he might just go ahead and buy that one of him. So we have our own pork now, tucking in even more stores for the winter.

Though my influenza did not linger, it left me out of kilter, so that Otis and I woke up in the night and, thinking it was just before dawn, got up and started the wash, which needed doing since I was not able to on Monday morning.

Otis started the fire in the yard and filled the pot, and I gathered the washing, but it seemed to be continuing dark and dark, the sunrise never coming though the sky was clear. Finally we saw some graying on the horizon and determined the time from that, laughing together that my watch wants repairing. No wonder we were so tired! We got to bed early that night, even DeWitt matching our plans, and next morning Otis set off to Ionia with nine axe-halves[24] he had fashioned. He returned with an axe in the afternoon, a yellow hound trotting alongside him. I walked partway down the road carrying DeWitt to meet him, and the dog pulled his nose out of the bushes and barked to startle me and make DeWitt cry. Otis called him back as he lunged toward us, the new master settling things with the dog. After a few words the hound calmed and Otis beckoned me forward to meet him. I like a good dog, once I get to know him.

When we all turned to the shanty again we saw a rainbow over the wood to the east, over Father's sugar-bush. It seems there's a nursery rhyme to be made of that, and we're jolly enough to make one these days!

---

[24] axe handles

*From the Journal of
Rosette Churchill
December 1857*

    Wednesday 9th. Some stormy. Otis went to Sol's raising A.M. came home to, [sic] carried De Wit to Ann's where I spent the afternoon. Otis ate supper there. Old Mr. Garter called. . . . They all ought to call him Sir Henry Garter I guess [,] though they are all quite . . . proud [--] . . . Otis' relatives.

    Wednesday 30th. I had such a stiff neck I could do nothing but take care of [DeWitt], & that with difficulty. Otis did the work. Ann called & borrowed some sugar. Frog Smith (as he is called) sued Otis again.

Solomon – Commerce

A S DECEMBER IS UPON US I am almost ready to raise my house, having set everything in readiness. I can spend the winter preparing it, then claim my bride in summer, bringing her to a place she can be mistress of as soon as we are married. Otis nods at my plans and perhaps has a bit of regret, being always hindered in the building of his new house by the claims of his new family. Rosette bears the strain, and cannot seem to see beyond the day before her, living one day to the next in the pressing needs of the moment. DeWitt is crying nearly every time I see him.

I went over there with Prince the first week of the month to invite Otis to my house raising, and Otis's yellow hound streaked down the path at us, with no good intent. Prince held his own, though, and they soon made a truce and then friends. By the time we got up to the shanty they were playing like brothers. Rosette told me they were calling the dog Blonday, after Brian Blonday in some adventure tale of theirs.

I found Otis's grandfather Henry Garter on the premises, he having brought back a gun he had borrowed.

He is a noble man of proud bearing, and I was honored to meet him. He, too, will raise his house here and be a solid addition to the community. After he left, Rosette said, "Well, Brother, what do you think of Grandpa Garter?"

"He seems a man like Father," I answered.

"Only more easy, at least to me," she said. "He was formal with you but has marked me for a grand-daughter right away and is very kind and smiling."

"That is nice," I said, "considering we have no other grandparents about."

"New York is far, and so is the grave," she answered, with a pause. "But this one doesn't want to be called Grandpa."

"What does he want to be called, then?"

"Old Mr. Garter!" she laughed. "But I don't see how he can help being called Grandpa when he has so many grandchildren. Do you know he writes a family letter from time to time? He told me of the one he wrote a few years ago, when Otis was working away for the first time—said both he and Sylvester were smart boys."

"He will approve of all your journal writing, no doubt," I said. She smiled.

Next day was my house raising day. Fourteen men and assorted boys answered my invitation. Father helped direct all the work, since when we raised the house on our farm I was just a boy, though I have taken part many times since. At last it is my turn, and we made a hearty crew, hustling to stay warm at first, then shedding our coats and hats as the day proceeded.

Each one took his task from me or from Father, then went to it with his own skill. When one wall was done we raised it with long poles and ropes, and once all four were secure we congratulated ourselves and fell to our dinner laid out by Mother. I appreciate my neighbors—ready and willing to pitch in each man to his neighbor's work. We are changing the look of this land a little at a time.

* * *

I wanted to put my house on a rise facing west, overlooking the creek and the bluff leading down to it. The creek runs along the south edge of Otis's farm, in his sugar-bush. I brought Jennette here the last days of school, when she was still with us, and she liked the idea I have for this place. We pretended for only a few moments that it was all speculation, and before I knew it I was facing her, taking her hands, and asking her to be my wife.

"I have written your father and he has agreed, so long as you are content to accept." Why was I suddenly so cold, so jittery, when all our time together before had been so easy? But she made it simple.

"Yes I will, and gladly," she said, smiling at me for a kiss. I obliged, taking her into my arms and drawing her soft breath and life into myself and giving her mine. When we parted, she looked around at the property we had just walked.

"It is lovely, Solomon. I will be proud to be mistress of this piece of ground, of this sunset. And of you."

I was undone and stammered, "W-we have our own sugar-bush right there to the south, adjoining Father's." My heart settled a little and I continued: "The creek winds through from Otis's spring along just there, and to ours and Father's. Then it turns north to join the Grand at Lyons."

"And you have some fish in it sometimes, don't you?" she asked. Her calm gave me calm. "I can just see a little boy like Frank or Jerome sitting on the bank of the creek with a pole. Can you not? Just there?" She pointed.

"Of course," I answered. "And I will make a blue door for you, as you once mentioned wanting, and pots for planting flowers on either side of the front stoop."

"I'm glad you know what is required of you," she laughed, running teasingly away, up onto the rise where the porch would go. "From our front porch, raised up on this little hill, we can watch the sunset day after day, year after year."

* * *

Much of our work was complete the first day, and each man walked off to his home, since all are close. Only my own family men—Father and Daniel Watson (who will soon be family) and Otis—were to return the next day, and then three days beyond would be Father's hog killing. I pledged to help with that.

The day we killed hogs was a family party, Rosette and the baby at Father's as well, and another warm and pleasant day, good for the work. Otis was digging of late—while the ground yielded. He told me he opened a new potato hole for winter storage and dug a watering trough for Mr. Barber. He is to receive a pork bowel for that. I hope Rosette gets Mama's sausage recipe and spice to make the best of it. She could not do better. I didn't get to speak to Rosette much, but purposed to visit with her a little.

"I've had an introduction to Grandma Garter," she said, wiping the scald pot steam from her face with her apron. "She's a fine old lady. But they have a dog that bit Sarah Maria on her cheek—opened up two places that bled for quite a while."

"I don't like a dog like that—always worries me when the beast comes out too easily."

"I know," she answered, "but Otis's dog seems all right."

"If he handles him well."

While we worked, Otis said he'd been out squirrel hunting and brought home four to eat. This is meat time, what isn't eaten or salted kept frozen until needed. Now that we were done at home, he was going to help his neighbor Long with butchering the next day.

Several days on I went with Father to ask Otis for help with my house again, and he was disturbed about a summons from Mr. Smith, for dogging his hogs, he said. Smith asked to let his hogs into Otis's woods and he allowed that, but then it seems Blonday got mixed up with them a time or two. At least that's what Otis says, though it would be pretty irresistible for a spirited fellow like him to be faced with some game to chase with that fine hound. Frog Smith is pretty irresistible to pester, for that matter. Next time I see Luther when I'm up near Lyons I'll have to tell him this tale of his father. Otis also got a summons from David Morse for goods bought on credit, but he has what is needed to settle that right away. Father agreed to go with him to town to see about the other.

"So," Father said when he got home, "Otis has non suited[25] Frog, so it is over for now."

"I suppose it's hard to prove whether a dog is doing dog business on his own or with encouragement," I answered.

"Just so. But I expect he'll serve him again soon," he said. "Frog Smith is not so easily deterred."

The little Churchill family met us at home for breakfast next day and we men went to work, while Mother took the horse and wagon with Rosette and the baby to a friend's for dinner. Next day Mother, in her best dress, sailed over to see Rosette, expecting to meet the vaunted "Grandma Garter," but somehow they were not able to come, so she was somewhat deflated in that, and came home directly. On Christmas she went back again, with another lady, just to see Rosette, Otis, and the baby.

---

[25] appealed for the dropping of a lawsuit

Later in the day Jerome trotted over to borrow Rosette's red dress for Ellen for a party that night. When he returned Jerome dumped the parcel with the dress on the table and complained, hands over both ears, "How that baby does cry all the time!"

"I don't know how to advise her," Mother told me. "None of you ever had such colic." She went for a visit and said he was the same, and Rosette laid up again with such a stiff neck Otis must do her work, though she could still care for the baby. It is not an auspicious close of the year for them, and, as we expected, Smith repeated his summons on Otis. That man is a nuisance.

1858 MICHIGAN

From the Journal of
Rosette Churchill
January 1858

Friday January 1st. 1858. Otis' 25th birth day & the 1st anniversary
of our wedding. Mother came for De Wit & self with the horse & cutter
(as my neck was about well) & took me home with her to spend New Year
evening, which is the first sleigh ride I have had this winter. . . . Danced
twice. Otis came to supper & we staid all night

Friday 15th. Otis & I & De Wit went to father's P.M. to see Cyrus
Packard & his wife. The latter is a speaking medium. . . . Mother invited
in several. Uncle M's family with exception of himself & Mr. Garter,
Colonel & wife, Mrs. Kinney, Anne & Ellen, the Mousehunt boys, J.
Utter, J. Jackson, Mr. & Mrs. Howe &c. were there to witness spiritual
manifestations.

Rosette - Medium

MAMA CAME FOR ME IN THE CUTTER this New Year day to be sure of a proper celebration, and we have indeed enjoyed it. Otis is a quarter of a century along now, and though I don't like to remind him he is younger than I, I made some "old man" jokes to him when we rose this morning. I think he is satisfied to be catching up in his age with how he feels in his mind, his thoughts on the next work to be done. So the baby and I whisked off home—or to Mama and Daddy's home—for a day of revels while Otis worked, though he would join us for supper and beyond.

The short sleigh ride was beautiful, reminding me of our wedding journey last year, when Otis drove furiously each day we traveled, to get to our next lodgings, some unknown place with unknown bed . . . and I his true destination. We would find our hosts' place for us, discover the lumps in the mattress or the scratchiness of the bed cloths, and cling together in warmth of two kinds. Once we had Aunt Lucinda's lofty quilt of down, like a cloud, that she put on our bed our wedding-night. But it was just borrowed, for then she took it back for herself and Uncle Myron and we made shift with ordinary quilts and batting after that. I would have done the same!

Travel mornings we gathered our things into our bags, laced and buckled up in our clothing and outer wrappings for the ride, and I would take leave of the woman of the house with little helps in the kitchen or smoothing the bed while Otis saw to the horses and hitched them to the cutter. He would usually heat bricks on a stove or in the fire to put at my feet. Then we would take ourselves off, our little traveling party removed to another spot on the map for another night, or a few, ourselves happily tired in body and cheerful in mind.

"What are you thinking of, Daughter?" asked Mother as we passed the McKelveys' on our way, our own place sinking away behind us with Otis chopping in the yard. "You seem gazing into nothing."

"Oh, it is nothing—just thinking of this time last year, on our wedding day."

"Happy times to remember—"

"Mostly," I answered. "It seems things do not ever turn out so well as we hope them to. I know Otis would—if he could—have us a house raised by now, and instead he has been raising Utter's the last couple of days, and Solomon's before that. And Solomon without even a bride yet to put in it!"

"Each in his own time," she answered. "But look at what you do have—a fine baby here, and mostly well, which is more than many can say."

"You're right, Mama. But when he cries so, all the time, it seems, I become so weary."

"He seems content right now, doesn't he?" she asked, peering into the blanket I wrapped mostly around his head. DeWitt's bright blue eyes looked out, keen with the cold. He likely enjoyed the rocking and thumps of the cutter, and the chinking of the fastenings. "When he is older, more able to get about, I expect he will be happier, though I don't know if you will," she smiled. "Those boys do get into trouble!"

Father's place was coming into view. Frank was scrambling around on the woodpile while Jerome set up for splitting some wood—small logs he could handle. Smoke streamed out of the chimneys, two of them, and evergreens draped the porch railing. That was Ellen's doing, what I might have done if I lived at home—a house set up for New Year.

Inside, I found all as usual, but more festive. Mother had baked and stewed for the party to come, and Ellen took DeWitt for me so I could help set up for dinner and then the supper. "Thank you for the loan of your dress, Rosette," said, settling the baby on her hip. "With hoops and extra petticoats it looked well on me."

"And not too short?" I asked.

"No," Mother answered, "as she is still small."

Dear Ellen, so overlooked most of the time, and worthy of being noticed. I ventured, "Ellen, would you like to wear it this evening, too?"

"Oh, could I?" she asked, face lighting up.

"Yes, I would like to see it!" It does not take much to brighten another's day, and why not do it when we can? I found the cutwork linen napkins we used for our wedding-day dinner and put them out again. As they had done for our wedding, Mother and Father invited all of Otis's King family and our now-dear friends the McKelveys. The day passed pleasantly and became more festive when Otis joined us. We even danced a time or two, and then took our baby and slept in my old room, on my old bed—it's a tighter fit with a husband AND a baby! But Mother could not remember where the cradle was, it's been so long without her needing it there.

In the morning Otis loaded us up in Father's cutter and left us at home before he went on to Ionia. Lorena

Howe and Dr. Gilbert came on a social call but looked DeWitt over as well, pronouncing him "fractious but fine." Good, then. I got word that Grandma and Grandpa Garter intended to come the next day, so I did the best I could with the meal. First Grandma came with Ann, and we had a nice visit, I even able to pretend to be a woman of leisure since I had prepared everything earlier in the day. Mama would be proud. Then "old Mr. Garter" joined us for supper. He gave some counsel when Otis told him of his plans to help Colonel dig a well, and Otis was uncommonly patient to listen, then philosophical later. "Grandpa is usually right in what he says," Otis said. "My father suffered—and our family with him—when he failed to heed him."

"I don't know your father," I ventured.

Otis darkened. "Not much to say of him."

"But I do hope to meet your mother someday," I said. I hope she thinks well of me from my ambrotype portrait Otis sent, and from the letters I write at his dictation. I add a bit of my own. "—And your brothers," I added.

"I'll send for them when our place is ready," he answered. "For a visit. Sylvester does most to keep up the place, and Henry George, even as a boy, was hard to manage."

Over the months I had pieced together little bits of Henry George's history—the fires he set, his rages and thrashings at meeting—and I trembled to think of what might ail him. But Otis did not like to speak of it.

"Perhaps a journey will be something for him to look forward to," I said. "And your mother would surely enjoy the change."

"Perhaps," he said, biting off the end of a leather binding he was using to repair his snowshoes.

I think Otis appreciates Father's help with the legal things—they went together to attend to Smith. I can just see Frog Smith cringing under the gaze of black-suited

Jacob Ramsdell, Justice of the Peace—though with no jurisdiction in this particular case—as Otis offered to settle. They carried four bushels of corn in the cutter—no more, lest Smith insist on all of it. I imagine Otis holding out a hand to drop coins onto Frog's table, for the cost of the lawsuits he'd taken out. They came home in triumph, joking together as Father let him out on our road and waved an arm to me in greeting before clicking at the horse. He eased the reins forward and glided off.

Another cousin, Edwin Ramsdell, is staying with Mother and Father for a while, looking out for a good farm. We are having visits between spurts of bad weather, he traveling about with Sol most days. Otis went over to borrow pork from Father. He limped up to the door a couple of hours later—swinging his body far out to one side with every step of the snowshoes, and groaned as he handed over the bundle.

"Five pounds, seven ounces," he panted in the doorway, grimacing as he unbound his feet. "Write it down." He keeps close accounts to avoid any question of what is a gift, what a purchase.

"Whatever is wrong with your legs?" I asked, offering my arm for support to bring him inside.

He waved me off and burst out—"Not legs—back. Oof!" He collapsed into the chair by the door and took off his boots, then climbed up into the bed and stayed there all the rest of the day. His eyes were closed in pain or sleep sometimes, and sometimes watching me. Once I put DeWitt up on the bed to play and his papa worked the baby's active arms and legs back and forth, both smiling just a little.

I made a pork and corn stew to keep us cozy, and heated a damp flannel to put on his back. By the next morning he must have been some better, because he went back out who knows where before Cousin Ed came for dinner with me. While we were eating and visiting we heard a commotion in the yard. I opened the door to see Frank all snowy up to the hips and down his cap, holding out a note from Mother.

Uncle Myron had invited Mother and Father, the McKelveys, and us to his home for the next afternoon. Mother arranged that I should walk to Ann's, and then she and Father would come along and take me and the McKelveys on to the Kings'. Otis walked with me most of the way to Ann's, carrying DeWitt, then he turned back to do his chores. But when I got to Ann's no one was there. I didn't know what to do and finally went on, stopping at Jackson Utter's house, where his boarder talked with me a little as we waited for Father. But time went on and no one came. Then Jackson arrived and offered to carry DeWitt for me as far as Mr. Kinney's, and I went the rest of the way with him myself. What a journey! Not far to walk, but a trek in the snow.

Just as I trudged into the yard Father was turning the cutter to come back looking for me. I must have misunderstood the time, for they were running late themselves, and when they found I was not at Ann's they went on, expecting I'd gotten ahead of them, and must have passed while I was inside at Utter's. Only Cousin Edwin arrived later than I, having walked from Mother and Father's by himself to leave room for us Churchills in the cutter. We were all in arrears but enjoyed ourselves just the same. We enjoyed cider and apples, then supper in the evening.

These frozen days, so short and dark, shut up in the shanty with the baby, it is a sweet pleasure to get out and about the neighborhood, and I am grateful.

* * *

The fifteenth we had an eerie experience. Jerome and Henry came by and invited the three of us to Father's that evening to see Cyrus Packard and his wife Betsy, a cousin I have only ever heard about and never met. Mother does not fully follow these spiritual notions of Cousin Betsy, but she seems drawn to them; Father so little credits them that he was not even in attendance, having found something else to spend his evening on. Father does say that Mr. Packard is a shrewd businessman, and the railroad station he plans in Lansing will, with the hotel next door, make his fortune.

The winter's teacher, Miss Mary Dodge, came to supper along with Ellen Badger, and they stayed on. Mother invited in several, including Uncle Myron's family, though Uncle Myron himself must have occupied himself with Father, because he was not with us, nor was Old Mr. Garter. But Colonel and Ann, Mrs. Kinney, and the Howes attended, with Jackson Utter and his boarder, the Mousehunt boys, and a couple of young girls with our Ellen.

The Packards had gone out for a stroll in the snow after supper, and all assembled at the appointed hour to await their return. The cheerful chatter of suppertime became a muffled murmur here and there as the folk sat uncomfortably peeping at one another or, like Otis, fiercely not peeping at all. We heard a shuffle at the door and mother hurried to open it. Cousin Betsy stepped in with royal poise while Mother eagerly reached for her deep gray hooded cape and draped it across her arm, turning toward the kitchen where tea cakes were moments from scorching.

Cousin Cyrus took his place standing against the wall at the back of the room and Cousin Betsy waded her way to the front, all eyes on her bare head held high, a dark veil dangling from her hand. She smoothly settled into the chair Mama arranged at the cloth-covered table, and with an imperious air placed the veil on her head and held both hands before her, palms up, then curled them toward herself, drawing us nearer about the table. With quiet care we lined up in three rows. Otis stayed in a rear row with me, Mother in the place nearest Betsy, her face flushed and pale alike in the lantern light. I saw tears lying behind her wide but downcast eyes, she thinking far beyond us. She was intent in hope that during the evening she would hear a word from beyond the grave, from dear Diana.

"We are all here to witness spiritual manifestations," Cousin Betsy announced, breathing mystery and certain knowledge into the room. I had heard of rapping, and Mother told me some of what Tarot cards are for—that is why she did not like my nine of spades quilt.

What transpired next was lost to me at first in the dark and whisperings, as Cousin Betsy drew all spirits toward hers, but DeWitt began to stir in my arms, and then to whimper, and I had to leave my chair. Shushing and jostling DeWitt, seeking to cover his cries with the rush of soothing words, and by that apologizing for the disturbance, I edged out past Cousin Cyrus, around the doorway, and into the hall. But Baby was not to be quieted and I retreated further.

Tucking my skirts into one fist and hoisting him higher on my shoulder, I climbed the familiar steps to my old bedroom, one slow step at a time. DeWitt quieted a little with the movement, looking about in the dark. The expectant silence, with Betsy's entreaties, swirled around my feet. Truth told, I was glad to have escaped it.

I knew DeWitt was full, so didn't offer to let him suckle, and I was careful not to turn his body in a way so as to make him expect it. But I brushed along the bed to the window, where, if I pulled back the drape to one side, I could see the half-round of the moon, the glow suffused in the surrounding cloud, a frigid halo sparkling around it. The light lay along the stubbled field, and ice glittered on the bare branches of the wood.

DeWitt looked with me, taking in the calm of our farm I had always loved. I gave him that, cooing—"And there is the barn, and horsies within . . ." He turned his round head at my voice, put up a chubby hand against my lips, nails scraping my teeth rhythmically, as if to clutch at the words that flowed from me. His own lips formed a bubble. We were secure here, away from the spirits Cousin Betsy conjured for the crowd below.

DeWitt latched his fingers in my hair, dragging out its smooth wave so a length of it draped over my shoulder. Never mind—I could arrange it again.

Mother was down there, hoping against hope to have a glimpse of Diana, who used to share this room with me. Could Cousin Betsy really call upon Diana, bring her spirit into this house again? I feared to see that, I thought, as I held my son to my neck, closing with what was real and safe. I felt DeWitt grow heavy on my shoulder, my pinned watch ticking beneath his ear, and turned back from the blue-bright window to the shadow of the room.

—And there she was! Diana, in a bonnet and cloak, on the other side of the bed, waiting quietly for me to turn. My heart pounded hard in my chest, my breath caught, and DeWitt stirred a little as I gripped him.

But as my thoughts clutched at me, my reason knew that it was not Diana, only some clothes hanging on the familiar old hook on the wall. My heart still pounded, but as when I finished climbing a hill, resting, not in the toil of doing it. How could I have been so silly? But I would not turn my back on the cloak and bonnet. Instead, I stepped out into the hall and closed the door, standing at the top of the stairs. I strained my ears to hear what passed below, but it was only the deep melody of Betsy's chants and appeals, a gasp, the creak of a chair or the table.

When all was done and DeWitt heavily asleep, I stepped quietly down the stairs and then into the room, and as the chairs scraped with everyone leaving, Otis turned to see me there. Later as we prepared to walk home again, I found the evening had become the source of a quarrel.

"I should not have taken part in those theatrics tonight," Otis complained, "And I wouldn't have if I had known your father would not be there, nor Uncle Myron. I felt like one of the young boys instead of a man who knows the way of the real world."

"But Otis," I answered, "No one made you come, and Jackson was there, and Colonel."

"You know Colonel McKelvey can be a real fool," he growled, speeding his walk so I rushed a little to keep up.

"You were curious," I answered. "Don't you want to open your mind to the spiritual, as Cousin Betsy suggested?"

"It's nonsense—'chaff,' Solomon calls it. And I feel a fool for being drawn in, while he and your father—and Grandpa and Uncle Myron—all kept themselves away."

"Mama means well, you know, Otis, and it pleased her for you to be there."

"Not worth my self-respect, I say, and you should not have set me in the way of that compromise."

"How was I to know, Otis, what would happen there?" I asked. "And besides, don't you think there just might be something to it?"

"Not to a rational man, and not to a religious one like Solomon. Not even he, pious as he is, wanted anything to do with it."

"It's not piety keeping you wary of it, is it, though?"

"No, of course not," he answered. "I am a man of realities."

"Are you?" I asked, hot. "You are a man of work, of advancement and solid gain, but I don't know what else."

"You do not do well to challenge me, Rosette. I demand respect."

"And you have it, for all you do," I answered, determined to speak my mind. "You have been a good husband and father, and I would never question that. But you do not appear to have strong ideas of what should be, beyond the wood and harvest and sugar—and our house."

"What would you have me do? I don't read your fancy *Journal of Education*, but I have read *The True Flag* that Sylvester sends, and I attend the preaching. I am not your father, nor Solomon for that matter."

"Nor would I have you be, Otis," I said more softly, reaching out to take the sleeping baby from his arms. "I do not know what I want myself. Mother has old folk ways deep in her family, and Cousin Betsy brings that out in her, but that is not for me."

"I think I know what is," he answered. "I think you are one like me—a hard worker who does things decently according to the precepts, but not carried away by the ether. You have shown me that. We agreed before we wed that we were by mutual consent more man and wife than what any words said by Elder Gown could make us."

"But those words are important, and I feared to call down judgment on us if we spurned them—not to mention the whispers of neighbors and frowns of family. If God has wrath, we do well to keep away from it."

"Does Cousin Betsy help with that?"

"I don't think so," I answered, "but I can understand Mother wanting to have any means she can to understand. And the hope of contacting Diana again—it is powerful."

"What is the grave, in any case?" he asked. "Just a hole in the ground—like McKelvey's well or our potato hole. It has a purpose to hide away a body lest it rot among us. But judgment after the grave? I don't think we need worry about that. This world is our reward, or our punishment. We make it ourselves."

"That's a cold wind to blow through my soul," I answered. "Let's leave off . . ."

"But you are making it well, Rosette. We make our own world, and we do well together."

"I think we do, and I want so to do well with you." I offered him the sleeping babe again, and our quarrel was over.

That conversation on our walk, that cold starry night, was one of the longest we've had. I think I came to know this husband more than I have known him before. His words did chill my soul, and leave me lonesome somehow. But when I think of all he does for me, for DeWitt, and his respect for my family, I am comforted. We will be well together.

Two days later, in the afternoon, I was surprised to see Mother and Cousin Betsy at my door. My first thought was gratitude that Otis was away at the Kings' and thence to Lyons with a few bushels of wheat. I welcomed the ladies into the shanty and gave them some cakes, made the day before, and cider from a jug the Howes gave us. Mother was proud to have a private audience with me and Cousin Betsy, who was influenced to pray, sing, and speak as she had the other night we saw her. She was praying, and that should be all right. She is a very smart woman, and good, I judge, pretty sure of that.

"Many of the spiritualists are strong in the Abolition," Cousin Betsy declared. Perhaps I will see what Father thinks of that. I did not tell Otis of their visit, determining not to bring it up but not to tell a falsehood if he asked. That should be all right.

A few days later I tried our lard, and it was fine, and Otis went to Mr. Barber's for a half barrel to store it in. I was surprised that Otis went to meeting on Sunday on his own, which is not usual for him. Perhaps he is thinking of what we spoke of, but I will not raise the subject, as our long talk, though important, was not pleasant. I think he would rather we did not do that again.

Dear Frank has brought DeWitt a book he made, and came over on his own, though I do worry about his walking all that way alone. Next day, he came again with Ellen and Jerome, and we had a little party with the carrots Mother sent with turnips and potatoes the day before. I cut them into sticks and we crunched away and danced them on the table like little dolls. It was silliness and good for us all.

As the month draws to a close it is time to chop sugar wood again, for us and for Father, so Otis is staying busy with his axe. His arms and shoulders are strong and solid, and I rub liniment into them of an evening. Those are good times between us, as he tells up how much wood and how many loads he has made, and the other accomplishments of his day.

From the Journal of
Rosette Churchill
February 1858

    Sunday 14th. More snow. . . . Father & mother spent the evening with me, & they are the first evening visitors we have had since we have been housekeeping.
    Monday 15th. A flurry of snow. Otis read in the evening Bryan Blonday, out loud as we generally do our reading.

    Wednesday 17th. Pleasant & cold. . . . The mice have gnawed the sock yarn so that it is a trouble to wind it. If I could have done as I wished I should have had a cat long ago.

Otis - Engagements

T IS WELL THAT THE SEASON for chopping is the season of the coldest weather, for it keeps me warm no matter the snow swirling about me. As long as my ears are wrapped up and my back turned against it, the wind is bearable. My shoulders work, the axe bites, and by the end of the day I have chewed through a good patch of woods or a big pile of logs. For a change I walk to Father Ramsdell's and chop for him, or vary my tools for a different kind of work— sugar wood, stove wood, house logs.

The wood is clean, the snow bright, and I am my own man, proving myself by the load I make at the end of a day. Sawdust and snowflakes whisk up in the wind, and I open flats and wedges with the axe, the tight splitting sound a satisfaction. As the sun dips below the treetops in later afternoon, if I am working at home, I put away my blades, unwrap my scarf, and stamp the snow off my boots at the door. Inside, most evenings, Rosette will have the supper ready, but I am nearly blinded in the dim shanty, only the flicker of the stove and lantern after the bright I have just come from. The closeness presses in on me—steamy musky frying or stewing, wet wool, and always the soiled wrappings of the baby. It's no place for me inside that cave of a place, nor for Rosette. I'm glad when I can help her visit elsewhere, get out of this dank hole. This summer I mean to have our house finished and a better place for us for next winter. Then we can use the shanty as another barn and get that cow.

The cold and the wind makes for the same kind of work each day, for each of us. My wife must keep all her work pressed in around her, where there is no room to turn around. She devotes a good part of the day to keeping the stove working, to warm her and the baby, and to properly cook our food. We have not so many bringing us things these days, so it is salt beef, parched corn, and all our good stored wheat, to keep us fed.

One day I came in a little earlier than usual, the sun still over the tops of the trees, and found DeWitt bolstered up in the rocking chair like a proper little man.

"Otis, see how well he sits there? I have kept him thus for something like two hours, and he has been happy and looking about him all the while! Hasn't cried at all!"

"Well, that is fine," I answered, pulling back a chair from the table. "I saw Grandpa out on the road, making his rounds, and he invited himself here for dinner tomorrow."

"It is a shame we do not have a fatted calf to offer such a distinguished guest," she said, mocking a curtsey.

"I suppose it is his privilege to rule us all, now he is here."

"And you will be just like him in your own time, wandering the roads to poke your nose in your grandchildren's houses to see what they are about," she laughed. "And with a carved walking stick, too."

"Perhaps." I stood before the stove to dry the backs of my trousers, then unlaced my boots to trade my wet for dry. "Do you have those new stockings started for me yet? The toe is out of this one now, and the heel very thin."

"I would have made a good start today, Otis, as I had the time, but I found the mice have been in my work basket and torn up the yarn."

"And so you will start in again about a cat, will you?" I asked.

"I don't know why I cannot have one. It would be a help with the mice," she said.

"I have heard that before."

"Have you thought about your grain? I've seen what the mice can do to an unsecured bin of wheat—"

"Mine are secured," I replied. "Or sold for ready money, or traded for flat-irons and such for you."

Rosette did not answer but bundled the baby up out of the rocker, where he had begun to slump, and set about to change his cloths. The lid pulled off the wash bucket sent a cloud of fumes into the room, and I gagged in spite of myself. "Don't carry on so," she bit at me. "This is only one day's cloths since I last washed. See my hands?!" She held them out, red and raw, me to see. "If I had a true kitchen as Mother does—"

"And as Ann does, and as Jennette will when she becomes Solomon's wife!" I shouted, my fist to the table to match my words.

"I only meant that I will be able to keep house better when I have a better house," she said, her voice lowered. "I know how hard you work."

"And are you glad we wed last winter, instead of waiting until summer or fall?"

"We could hardly have done otherwise," she answered, holding DeWitt before her to face me.

I did not answer, but stuck my still-damp feet back into my boots and slammed out the door for another load of wood. That night by the stove, as the wind and snow whirled around outside, I saw the swift dusky furtiveness of a mouse along the wall, but I resolved myself against Rosette's sigh. I won't have a cat fouling the wall of my home with his spray, pulling back his flesh to fang at me. As if a by-the-bye, she remarked, "Mother's Cloud is all sleek quiet, and deep purring in the lap."

"You haven't heard me, Rosette," I told her. "We will NOT have a cat."

"Then you might not have stockings this winter," she replied, holding up the mass of yarn bits stuck with husks and droppings. "The wee folk have had their way with this lot."

Next day, after few words between us at supper, none at bed, and only a grudging one or two when we rose, I could not open the door. In the night the snow had blizzarded in whirling masses wherever the wind pleased, banking up against the shanty. The warmth of the stove seeped through the logs to melt some, and then, in the early hours with the stove cold, the melted snow had solidified and locked the door tight. I had to lean my whole body through my shoulder against the door and then pull back to loosen the ice, scraping boots on the floor boards. But with main force I broke the seal and pulled the door open into the shanty. The wall of ice and snow outside was up to my waist.

I crawled up over the barrier, then felt my way and dug down with my bare hands to where I had left my axe. I crawled back inside and chipped away at the ice, flinging it out into the yard, hacking and pushing clots of ice and wet snow away from the shanty. I cleared it all the way to the road for Grandpa's arrival for dinner.

Then, without a word to Rosette and without my breakfast, I was off to Colonel's house—we are working together to get logs to the mill. Give me a job that needs work, and I can meet it, see my way to the next thing.

I delayed my arrival at dinner, to let Grandpa arrive first, but not late enough to seem disrespectful. I could hear them laughing as I brushed off snow outside the door, using Grandpa's walking-stick to knock the clots off my boots. "Welcome, Grandpa," I said as I came in, pulling off my hat. He rose to shake my hand.

"Good to see you, Grandson. Your pretty wife has been entertaining me, and my great grandson there has been sleeping, though I don't know how with all the chatter we have made." Rosette had thin braids pinned up around her head and leading to the knot at the back—very nice. Her cheeks were pink from the laughing, from the fire. I smiled at her.

I took the breadboard she held out to me for the table, and we set things right between us with it. It takes only a smile and a little task to make things right.

When he left an hour later, the light had grown dim, and the flying snow bit hard as it rushed in the open door. Nevertheless, the Ramsdells came calling after supper. We manage to entertain even in a small, close house—and Rosette knows how to make the best of what we have.

Next day all was really well between us, I think, and we spent our evening reading—or I read aloud as she knitted and cared for the baby. It is the dashing Bryan Blonday whose adventures we enjoy again, and we cannot help crying "Huzzah!" to one another for a lark, as they do so much in the book. She says Jerome and Frank will like playing at that when we share it with them.

Father Ramsdell came to see if I could loan him my cross-cut saw, which I sharpened and took over, then spent the evening with them and brought it back through the cold quite late. Rosette had already gone to bed, but a little warmth lingered in the cooling stove.

I am chopping out south of our place now, close to my sugar-bush to reduce the hauling for when we sugar off, though it is so cold I cannot imagine the sap running for many weeks yet.

* * *

No sooner had I thought that about the warming than the weather turned, and it is moderating indeed. Those cold nights and warm days are just what is needed to pump up the sap for the taps. As we waited for that I was going on errands for Rosette, fetching buttermilk and flour from her parents'. Then I took thirteen bushels of wheat to clean in Ramsdell's big barn, and stayed for Mother R's dinner. They wanted me to return next day to help fix a shed for Mr. Howe, but Colonel had promised to help me saw logs first. I planned to keep him right on the task—I had Rosette pack us dinner for our work in the woods.

I came back mid-afternoon from the sawing and was preparing to set out for Ramsdell's when Wellington Long ran over from their place yelling, "Fire!" I grabbed a pail of water and ran over, finding only the wood piled around the stove blazing up, so I threw it out into the snow. I asked where his parents were, and he said they had left him on his own. It is good I was home for just that need!

With the weather warming up, Rosette wanted to visit Ann for a morning, so I carried DeWitt over there for her. When we arrived Ann told us of a spelling school they were holding that evening, to mark the last day of the winter school. I agreed to meet them at Uncle Myron's at supper and go to the event, though it is not my way to spend an evening.

At supper I found that many of the ladies were at the school that afternoon, including Mother Ramsdell, since Father Ramsdell is one of the superintendents. And then we added men in the evening for an exhibit of the children's compositions and readings. Rosette said it was well done for new beginners, though I would not know. But most surprising was that Rosette spelled down the whole lot of us! She fairly burst with excitement as she bounced DeWitt on her hip and called out the spellings in a voice of command I have not heard her use before.

From the Journal of
Rosette Churchill
March 1858

    Thursday 11th. High winds. Otis . . . staid the evening at fathers &
brought home De Wit mittens that Marian Richardson sent him by Em.

    Saturday 13th. Otis tapped 106 trees.
    Sunday 14th. Rainy & warm. Otis worked in the sugar-bush.
    Monday 15th. Rainy & very warm. Otis borrowed a barrel of
Cornelius Mc. K. to smoke our hams & chops in, & smoked one ham. De
Wit has got well. The end of this Journal.

Rosette - Settlement

AND HERE WE ARE AGAIN at sugar time, in preparations for that. Otis drawed logs for firewood with Colonel's oxen and then spent the next day making sixteen sap troughs, then more the next day, too. He is determined to increase our yield, and with a home of our own near the bush we should not get lost again as we did last year. It is pleasant now to think back on the adventure, but I know we were a bit afraid at the time, or I was. I prefer my warm home and quilt-covered bed, tired as I am of the dark and closeness of it these days. It is strange to think that I have not been to town in over a year, though it is not far. I wonder whether I will go again or whether, like Mother, I have all I can see to here.

Last week Otis took wheat to Father's to clean and yesterday drawed home on their hand sled a bag of flour and one of bran, one of potatoes, and a jug of buttermilk. I used that to make a light bran bread for us, with cider-cooked dried apples. Only fresh cream could have improved it. Poor DeWitt has a cold that has settled on his lungs and makes him bark so—it would be funny if it were not worrisome.

The children cheer us when our thoughts grow dark. Jerome and Frank came to fetch the hand sled, and I had hard work of it to keep DeWitt inside with me instead of letting him go on a ride with them—they begged so. This time, in the next year or two, DeWitt will be his own little master of such adventures. While they were here Otis came out of the sugar-bush, his dog lolloping beside him, and asked Frank if he could count all the troughs he had made. I watched as he scampered to the task, holding up his fingers, stopping and starting a couple of times. Jerome sagely stood back, and I could see him counting in his own mind.

"Thirty and three!" Frank called in triumph.

"A score and thirteen," Jerome added.

All is ready.

While we waited for the weather to turn, Otis went to Aunt Lucinda, who gave him a hen and a rooster, which he carried home, one under each arm. "I call them Fanny and William," he announced, after Fanny Campbell, the pirate heroine in our book, and her love. She sailed from Massachusetts, and so did we, in a manner of speaking. Father's people, and the Churchills, too, set out from New England to New York a half-century and more ago, and thence to Michigan.

"What revolution will they will be leading?" I asked. "Huzzah!" Otis smiled and ducked into the lean-to to fashion a pen for the birds, but not before he chucked them into the shanty for the time being. Something more underfoot—it is no matter.

Eggs will be nice when we have them.

1866 MICHIGAN

Solomon - Departures

SEPTEMBER A DECADE AGO I rumbled along in a wagon on this road, carrying Rosette to the Teachers' Institute in Lyons. But today on horseback I turn west instead, toward Ionia, skirting it on the south, to follow the Grand River west, then north to Grattan—to my farm and my children, thirty miles and a lifetime away.

Behind me is my first home, the house we raised together those glad December days in 1857—Father, Otis, my friends and neighbors, my brothers and the other boys drawn to the task. Jennette's blue door, looking west to the sunset. Such happy times we knew there together when we took possession as man and wife that summer, claiming our joy. From that doorstep we could see the neighbor children on their way to school and think of our firstborn, Seymour, doing the same, then Callie and whatever other babes would follow. Mother and Father were prospering on their adjoining farm, and Rosette and Otis on theirs, our babies' births alternating and weaving a fabric of life. This was our land, our home.

* * *

When Lincoln won the election in 1860 I was proud that Father had heard him speak for Frémont in Kalamazoo in 1856, Lincoln's only time on our soil. We took up that cause, to cleanse our land of slavery by first preventing its spread. A man must work his own land to rightly own it, and the Lord would not long bless our land worked by means of slavery. We knew from the papers and the talk of those who traveled back East and South that war was coming. I wanted to live quiet, but I knew my duty.

Great grief struck our family in 1862, when Rosette's little ones were smitten with a fever. Eva, a bright bird, had flaming cheeks herself the day her infant brother Frank was taken from us, and she succumbed a week later. We gathered to put their little bodies in the ground near Keefer's, and the Churchills laid a stone with both of their names on it. DeWitt was spared, and clung to Otis while Rosette became quiet, pale, and still for long after.

In 1863, when James Kidd was mustering troops for a second time in Ionia, after the battle of Gettysburg, I determined to go, to defend my people, my land, and to stand up for my votes. First I must care for my family, though. Otis was doing well with his land, content to work his prosperity from its immediate yield. But Father and Myron King saw the railroad voted out of Orange Township and laid in to the north, and were not willing to give up its prospects. Father sold his farm and set up in Lowell, turning his hand to trade, which was always the best part of his work. And the Kings traded farms with Samuel Riker, his in Vergennes, on the busy post road from Lowell to Grattan. Those westerly lands are sweeter, the hills more lush than our flat fields in Orange.

With war shaking our foundations, and our best neighbors gone, our land here seemed not so promising as before. I could not decide what to do for our future. If I returned from the battlefields, I could work our familiar fields and sugar-bush and perhaps extend to Father's adjoining, if the new owners would sell one day. Jennette and Rosette could care for one another as sisters, mingling the children in a little flock. If we left, there would be only Rosette's one boy, and the new child she was carrying.

But if I did not return, what would become of my bride? I decided to close up our place for the duration of the war—not many were looking to rent—and then decide. I knew Williams, just south of me, was eager for my place. So we left our farm after harvest, butchering and selling most of the animals, and I took Jennette, Seymour, and Callie to her parents in Grattan. Mother and Father would be nearby, to the south, and they could visit occasionally. I saw them settled and said my farewells, then saddled my best horse and retraced the roads. In Ionia I joined with the 6th Cavalry the last day of the year.

In 1864 we Wolverines were glad to lend our strength and skills that had broken up the land of Michigan to break up the land in the East. Marching and drilling were new work to us farmers, but we knew how to pull together, and we soon learned our duties. We built bridges and roads we needed and blasted those we didn't. My bugle called us to our work and to our cots and then up and out of them again, more shrill than any rooster, more bright than any dawning sun. We climbed over winter-fallow fields softening up sooner than at home and trod through weeds in war-fallow fields of men gone to war themselves, or dead. Our horses churned the soil, and too much our blood fortified it. I often thought of David running over mountains in his battles against the king whose troubles he had soothed with his harp. Our conflict, too, was personal, though I knew no rebels by name.

I saw famous battles—the Wilderness, Trevillian. I read of them when I returned last year. My bugle called men into formation and signaled them to fire, and sometimes I fought alongside the rest. I was captured in Virginia, at Trevillian, then sent to the perdition of Andersonville. I expected to see camps like those in the north—with men in a kind of idleness that was torture. Nothing to do, day upon day, but wander in the dirt, in ill clothing, with poor provisions. But Camp Sumter— Andersonville—was beyond imagining—men packed sickly one upon another, a swamp for a latrine, unspeakable disease and death. It was only God's mercy that I was transferred to Florence, South Carolina before many weeks elapsed.

My strength and earlier good food, my having been just half a year in training and combat—all these kept me whole. Or mostly whole—none of us was well in that place. But with only crippling rheumatism and bowel troubles, I got off easier than most.

A year after my capture I was home again in late spring of 1865—home being wherever Jennette might be. We fell into one another's arms with relief and gratitude to God. My return sapping my last strength, I was ill for many weeks. I still am, truth be told—I spy out every privy wherever I am. Though I try to do without it, sometimes I need a cane for my lame hip. Once I was able, I could help a bit with Father Watson's harvest. Persuaded to linger in Grattan yet longer, from time to time I went to Lowell to help Father with his saddlery—to rest my soul.

There was not to be full sweet rest, though, as we lost Mother this January. Otis and Rosette came in a cutter with the children, and though we were all shocked and mourned, and worried for Father, we knew somehow he would be well. He said she had spoken of a premonition of her death, and in a strange way that prepared him. "The Almighty has led me in the Word and in the meditations of the night to places of comfort," he said, anxious to assure all his children. His burden of loss will come slowly to him, over months and years, I expect, portioned out as he is able to bear it.

I did not plant in Orange this spring, my spirit hesitating somehow to return.

In March I rode down to the farm one day, when the Churchills were sugaring off, and joined right in, my horse tied up in Otis's sugar-bush. It was good to do the old work, though I did it as if an old man, decades aged beyond Otis. By silent pact we did not discuss the war he had not gone to. No need for that. "How is the sugar business this year, Brother?" I asked.

"Doing well," he replied with matter-of-fact cheer, as if he'd last seen me a day or two before. "I'm up to Father Ramsdell's quarter ton and more. We keep a little store in the old shanty behind the house, and a sign brings custom right to our door."

"But you take it to town as well, don't you?" I asked.

"Yes, and Rosette signs her fancy 'R-C' on the packets, to signify Ramsdell-Churchill, and our connection to the family. They know our sugar by that and ask for it especially." He hefted another armful of wood into the fire as I stirred up the syrup with the wooden paddle.

"How is Rosette, then? Jennette worries that she does not write. Does she miss Mother much?"

"So it is," he shrugged. "She has the house and children to see to, and less visiting than when you all were here."

The silence lay heavy between us. His guilt, my uncertain plans, the fact of what had passed. I broke the quiet with some little thing and then excused myself to go on to Rosette. I led my horse through the field path from the wood, admiring Otis's good care of his land. I looped the reins over a fence and came up to the door of the kitchen, as had been my habit when we lived catty-corner across two fields. I helped raise this house the summer Jennette and I married. I knocked and called out, "Any sugar for sale here?"

"Why Sol, I did not know who would be coming to my back door!" she said, opening the door with little Ella on her hip. The child buried her head against her mother at sight of me. "But I knew your voice at the first moment." Rosette's voice quavered atop the stirrings in her heart.

I stepped into the kitchen and kissed her brow, then wrapped my arms around her and Ella all at once.

"Oh, Sol, I am so thankful you have come back," she sobbed a little. "I could not speak of it when Mother passed, but I was determined to say it when next I saw you. I prayed for your safe return as I have never prayed for anything else in my life, save the children."

Grief again welled up between us. But this was a day to be glad. I made much of Ella, like Eva at her age, and all the more precious for that. When DeWitt, eight now, returned from his errand up to Riker's—what was the Kings'—with the old yellow dog Blonday, we were cordial. He speaks less than my Seymour—who is just six—how I wish they could grow up together! DeWitt is perhaps a touch sullen. I gave him a sweet Jennette had wrapped up especially for him, and to Rosette a fragrant soap with lavender such as Jennette was known for.

Ah! Jennette!

We enjoyed a good visit, and I stayed the night, sugaring off with Otis until almost midnight. I told him I was not yet firm in my purpose about the farm, but persuaded I should sell and settle in Grattan. "The land is good—"

"As is ours," he countered.

"Yes," I agreed. "But Jennette is so happy with her sister and family up there, and it is closer to Father. My only regret is to leave your company."

He looked up to search my face a brief moment, then bent back to his work. "We will be all right," he said. "I am prospering here."

"You are indeed." We did not mean to deceive, but we stopped short of the truth.

He needed me for his temper and vision; he needed Jennette for Rosette. And we them—for all the companionship of young people—kin—at good work together. I spent the return ride to Grattan silently chanting in turn, "We shall return to Orange. We shall remain in Grattan. We shall return to Orange—" until it was just syllables of nonsense in my mind and my thoughts all confused.

Just weeks later Jennette was delivered of a new blessing for us, baby Nettie, named for herself as Callie was for her sister. Perhaps that was what I was waiting for to make my decision. We would stay one more winter in Grattan and then go back to Orange. They needed us.

But the Lord had more than war and prison to add to my sufferings. Just as she should have been fully up and about after the baby, Jennette herself fell ill and then before we knew it was gone. Wind swept through my soul, scouring my bones, stripping away the flesh that had just begun to grow again. I could know only brief mourning, for the children needed me. Calista became aunt-mother to Nettie right away, so I needn't worry, but Seymour and Callie were sorely wounded, and I could not indulge myself at their expense. I decided to stay in Grattan.

* * *

Having arranged the sale of the farm to Williams from afar, I returned to Orange Township today after seeing to some final things in the county courthouse. Our old house was empty as my soul was empty. It is a mercy I do not have to see that house every day, to live in the kitchen she graced, to sleep in the bed we shared with its view to the east and the sunrise. While things were dry and stark within me was a good time to be done with the business, so I took leave of my house with the blue door.

Again I rode up to Rosette's back door and climbed those steps, having crossed catty-corner from my house for the last time. Otis was nowhere about, but Rosette saw me coming and just flew out the door into my arms. She had come on the train for Jennette's burial, leaving the children with Otis, but all was so stirred up then, and I so numbed, I did not even properly see she was there. Now was our time to mourn together, and we clung to each other on those steps for a long minute. We sat down right there, looking to the south, across Otis's fields, my house just visible—and the blue door.

"Solomon, I know you must stay in Grattan now," Rosette said bravely, the corners of her mouth trembling. "I know it is best for the children, and I know Jennette's people will help you. I had so hoped—but there is no help for it now."

I held my hat in my hands between my knees and listened. I knew she was right, and I was glad she was saying it. She gave me my liberty.

"And we will not be so alone," she smiled. "The Rikers have been good neighbors, and Arthur Mathews is settling in well at Father's farm since last year, buying more beyond the fifty acres he first bought. And that's not the only thing to keep us company. We expect another babe before the year is out."

I bent her head to kiss it, the deep cares of our life of the last decade softening to sweet affection the teasing playfulness we shared when young. Another baby—that would bring cheer to our family circle in the midst of such sadness.

When Otis came he clasped my hand and put a hand on my shoulder more intimately than he ever had before, in that touch saying what he would never say. Perhaps he offered in silence whatever I might find most comforting for myself, answering my awkward care for him when his little ones were carried off years ago. I knew deep assurance to draw from, as Father does, to ease our way in grief. Otis does not have that, and Rosette perhaps only a small measure. But I must leave them, entrusting their care to God.

1910 MICHIGAN

DeWitt - Legacy

MY LIFE IS CURSED. From the time I was a boy I have known only hard work on the farm and failed prospects. Pa made me chop and dig and slave on the farm until I was old enough to be on my own—and then some. With no brothers to help, just the girls for all those years, I got more than my share of the work. It was spare and lonesome at our place, and Pa off to town every opportunity. I was seventeen before Ma got a boy that could grow up—and another ten years until he was any good for the work.

Even when I was a married man—married to Lillie—I was chained to this place. But I got us away from here to Dakota Territory to try my hand on a farm of my own. Things there went against me, too, including Lillie. She stuck it out just ten years, through the 80s, even though I brought Ma there to help. After a few years Ma got too old for Dakota farm life and moved up to Fargo to my sister Ella and her husband Frank Paine. In town Ma could have her prim and proper household just like she wanted it.

Lillie was always pestering me to move us back to Michigan, so finally I gave up the farm and brought us all home to her mother. After Pa got shut of Ma and her proper ways and married that German woman, Barbara, they sent crazy Uncle Henry George to the asylum in Pontiac. I know Ma didn't like him and was glad we had a dog for when she was alone with him, but Pa just laughed her down: "Harmless!" he'd say. "He won't hurt anybody."

"But I don't like it—don't like him about the place with the girls here."

"I'm sure they can defend themselves," Pa told her. "And he's my responsibility, which you are bound to share."

Grandma Betsey Churchill died, my sisters married, and only my little brother Percy was left. I threw in with Pa and them for a while—I thought in the prime of my manhood in my forties, with Pa in his sixties, I'd have an advantage. But they weren't exactly grateful to have me.

Pa expected me to do all the work—kept reminding me it was my inheritance, by rights of me being the oldest son. That kept me going a year or two, but I wasn't near as fast as he was, and I couldn't wield the blades—axe nor plough—the way he did. When I saw how it would be, I went back to South Dakota for another try, then Lillie sued me for divorce from back here in Michigan—and what could I do about that?

My luck had no end of bottoming out. Along about 1902, Ma was sitting up there in North Dakota well taken care of by Ella, and got notice that some relative in Minnesota—Aunt Susan—had died and left her and some other female relatives each ten thousand dollars! I remember when ten dollars was a lot of money, and I don't think we ever saw a hundred dollars. I didn't expect to get a lot—Ma doesn't approve of me much. But I was scraping on that second South Dakota farm, or what should have become a farm, and could have used a boost.

Ma did send two hundred dollars from the legacy. It was something, but not nearly what she should have spared me, her oldest son, with just the start of a new farm of my own.

South Dakota is a hard place, and the two hundred dollars didn't go far, so I came back to Michigan again a couple of years later. I knew the German woman had died—and got buried with her first husband and under his name. Guess she didn't want to stay attached to Pa any more than Ma did. I wanted to know what Pa was doing with the place—what should by rights have been MY place. And what did I find? Pa had sold our farm and set up in a little house south of Ionia. He installed another stepmother, as well.

I told Pa about Ma's legacy so I could see him sputter and fume. But he smiled sly at me—I couldn't get him that way. Because I couldn't make the farm go in South Dakota, that's proof enough to him I didn't deserve to take over his farm here. But he hasn't been to Dakota—he doesn't know what you have to do when you don't have all these trees just pouring out their sap, for one thing. In Dakota there's prairie dog holes, and a wind that has a hundred miles' running start, and nothing to slow it down.

But I kept quiet and moved in with the old couple. I thought we'd have some loosening of the protocol, in a manner of speaking, and a man could relax.

That's what I get for thinkin'.

Sarah, the new wife, didn't like me around. But Lillie and the brood didn't want me back, either—they got by somehow in Church Alley in Ionia. I felt cast away, the way old Uncle Henry George was—after all those years lurking about the place.

And Pa, old as he was, still had all his arm strength, and started blacksmithing, taking over Sarah's Pa's and first husband's trade. Swinging the axe and digging with that plow all those years set him up to move right smooth into that profession.

But that didn't leave anything for me—the blacksmithing outfit didn't need me, and what's a lifelong farmer gonna do in a little house in town?

Percy was a barber, so I took to hanging around in his shop, telling stories of South Dakota to the men who came in. Percy liked it—good for business—and I could tell tales, some of them from those novels Pa used to read aloud of a night. Pirates, soldiers, cowboys—I knew 'em all. I paid attention to the barber trade, and did some of it, though I didn't have the school-trade learning Percy did. Nope—no special trade for dear son DeWitt.

When the census people came around a few months ago, Pa bragged to me that he'd cleaned Ma clear out of his life—told 'em Sarah was my ma! He started the thing in 1900, by telling 'em the two of them had been married for forty-three years. Well, he HAD been married for forty-three years, more or less, since 1857. Hardly done with one wife before he got another. He loves putting one over on the authorities. Guess I got a bit of that from him—cut from the same cloth, so to speak. Didn't get much of Ma in me.

So here I am, in a town homestead in Ionia, close quarters with Pa and Sarah—the old people—and me not knowing what to do with myself, proper. The land lost me out there, Pa lost my land here, and Ma could have saved me something but didn't. This family is eating itself alive and grinning over the gorge.

1913 NORTH

DAKOTA

Rosette - Winter

'VE ORDERED THE GRAVESTONE now for my firstborn, and that is not how it should be. Long ago I got used to it with the stones in Orange Township for the others, but once they're grown they should hold their places until we old ones are gone. Six of my nine children are in the ground, and their father, too. And I soon will be.

Poor Frank, named for his uncle, gone just after his first birthday, then Eva the next week, stronger at almost three but unable to survive the fever. Five-year-old DeWitt was spared. In those dark days the war came, and even as Solomon joined the cavalry and traded his fiddle for a bugle, Otis slipped away whenever the draft came near. I began to know shame then.

Two years later God sent me daughter Ella for a comfort, and she has been that for me here in Fargo, and my grandchildren. A consolation. Dora and Ida were strong daughters, too, though remote over the years with their own lives, glad to get away when they could. And what was there in Orange for them? With the war everything changed. Father and the Kings started new enterprises to the west after the railroad opened up Lowell. And when—thanks be—Solomon returned from the war, I thought we would have him and sunny Jennette and the children with us. But that was not to be, either. They all left me there, with shirking Otis, our fine farm and pleasant house hiding the truth.

Next I had Otto and lost him in the night, a tiny life that seemed darkened and constricted from its first moments among us, bringing such a pall with him that I dared not let myself love him. But I did in any case—how can a mother help it?

Percy, my youngest, is thirty-nine now—I can hardly believe it! Married to Ethel, but from daughter Ida's letters not happily. Will our family know the dishonor of yet another divorce, to add to ours and DeWitt's? He wasn't brought up to know happiness with a wife. His father has not shown him what it is to be a proper man, a man like his Uncle Solomon, or his Grandfather Ramsdell, or even Great-Grandpa Garter, who died long before he was born.

And then in those waning years of childbearing, dear Cressy came. Sweet and lovely as a doll—the girls played with her like one—until suddenly that terrifying cough took hold of her. She barked and strangled day after day, and finally she was carried off, as well.

At least my heart was able to love her, not too afraid to do so, and she brought a blessing to us all, even bitter Otis and his rough shadow, DeWitt. How I loved to spy that young man in his best days. As his father was with me, he was hopeful and happy, just a bit. He and Lillie set out for Dakota Territory, and welcomed their daughters the next two years. I was glad for opportunity to come out here to them when I could not bear my life in Michigan anymore. The Dakota farm seemed a refuge for me from all the darkness of Otis, and I was glad to be there when little Gaile was born into the worst January storm anyone has ever known in those parts—the Children's Blizzard. We were making it. Then things began to go wrong.

* * *

I see my idle hands in my lap, skin waxy and smooth—not like those many years red and raw. I remember when my hands were soft and young, occupied only with a needle and books, smoothing down my hair and tying my corset for a dance . . .

* * *

DeWitt found no resting place. That land would not yield to him, and Lillie tried to make do but at last persuaded him to return with the children to her mother in Michigan. I came to daughter Ella then in Fargo. I had nowhere, no one, to go back to in the east.

It all ended wrong for DeWitt. He dragged back to South Dakota alone after a while, then east again, back to Otis. Then my firstborn son, in his fifties, did not know how else to land himself, when his father died last year, but to fetch up to his mother's doorstep again, once more out west. Otis left everything to Percy—a pocket watch and an automobile. To the girls the silver spoons, and a feather bed for Ida. To his wife Sarah a wagon and team. DeWitt got nothing. I had little to offer him, having given all the children and grandchildren their portions of the legacy, and holding back what I needed for myself. My landlady gave DeWitt a room in the boarding house where I am kept. He, too, needed keeping.

So this was our home—these narrow rooms up wooden stairs, grimy windows letting onto Main Street, Fargo. Mother used to complain to Father of our being so far out of town, and having to build the road ourselves. Otis did some of that work, and Father and Sol, and even the little boys—they made our way. Now I am in the center of a town, a railway journey from our old farm, across the onetime wilderness.

The trains stopped with us in Michigan in those days. It was the edge of the wilderness, but one thickly peopled with friends and cousins. Here I sit in rooms on Main Street, with money in the bank and a cat on my lap.

I had hoped so much for a home like Mother and Father's, and we started well enough, with good land and much help from family and neighbors. We enjoyed good days, and Otis showed strong promise. He surely knew how to work hard! But hard is a good word for him. He lacked the warm dignity of Daddy, the confident rest of Solomon. My brother could light out to build his house, knowing he'd chosen the right girl to fill it for him. But Otis must secure the girl first, make her his without any possibility of turning back, then set about to build a house around her. We carried our young marriage with us from house to house that first year, as the babe DeWitt grew inside me, and we hastened to gather our household effects.

There's nothing that hexes a marriage begun a little out of order but the characters that set those patterns wrong to begin with. Many do well who have a baby just months after the wedding, but I wonder if I didn't allow the marriage to just catch me lest I be alone. But no, many start with people too young or hard-hearted or just foolish. The griefs and joys that come with sharing a bed and a household—and the children that follow—can shape those people, bringing maturity, wisdom, softness. They bring whatever is needed. I have watched Frank Paine and Ella over the years, and they have grown into one another, keeping his parents in their home, and me, and their growing children, and always keeping their poise and warmth. Frank gave Ella what we could not, so she has continued her growing with him. They weather the storms together and enjoy the sunshine together. Otis and I did not learn to do that.

He brought me grief and shame over the years, things I could not share with others for fear of even more shame. His failures made me a failure, too, for having assented to our marriage. No, more than that—for having chosen him for a husband.

Oh, the pain I feel to think of those words in my Journal 14. January 1, 1857. How naïve I was when I wrote the happy version of that marriage-day entry all those years ago. Even worse, how bitter I was when I changed the words later, in DeWitt's sod house a hundred miles south of here. What a pitiful old woman I was, old before my time, even before my looks caught up. I've had sufficient time to change in these eighty-three years. I thought my life was over when I saw my marriage was lost, but I've survived it by many years.

And what has sustained me? Well, certainly Ella and her brood—and Frank's good-natured patience with this old woman. But ties back home, to what I have loved most in my life—these have kept me, too. We used to visit so much back and forth in Orange Township and beyond, and write people when we could not visit. I knew Jennette Watson only for visiting when she kept school there, though I was drawn to her. But once she became Solomon's wife she took me on as her ward, though I was older. I revealed a kind of uncertainty, and she set to try to pull my thoughts together, to galvanize me. I knew a little proverb here, a list of rules there, having a vague sense of God's judgment that hung over me in gloom. But I could not make them work together in my heart.

Then came war, and the deaths, and the railroad that changed everything in a flash. Our little township was set as farms, and no more, from that time on.

That is when Jennette began to write to me, the year and more Sol was away. First he was in Custer's company in all manner of engagements Otis read to me about from the papers, then he became a prisoner. We didn't realize that with his return came Jennette's end. She conceived, then came to deliver the baby safely, but lost her life when we thought all would be well. But I saved her letters, knowing they were precious even as my eyes were blinded to what she longed to convey. She wanted to share her joy, her confidence—but they rolled off me as water beads and rolls off an oiled cloth.

After Mother and Jennette were gone, Father and Solomon—so dear to me—formed new bonds with new wives. They withdrew more fully from my life, and away from Otis. They could not help him be the man he should have been. We were left alone in Ionia County.

It is easy to see why Solomon chose Calista to follow Jennette in his heart. Of course she of all women could care most lovingly for her nieces, his motherless children—she glowed with her sister's beautiful spirit. These women, and my brother, and by all accounts their seven living children—knew the special mark of divine favor on their lives. It is not that they were especially lucky or had all the right charms Mother would have liked to furnish them with. It is not even that they were chosen by God because they managed to pull together what I have not. I know Solomon suffered from the war, from his wounds, and from his grief. No, instead, it is that they always have confidence that they walk in God's favor, no matter what their circumstances.

I have lived my life working hard to prove myself, and never believing I've hit the mark. It is clear from the shambles of my marriage and my sons' marriages that our family has missed something somewhere. But while there is life there is hope, as Father used to say.

That is why I welcomed dear, hard, bewildered DeWitt to my rented rooms here in Fargo last year. He came to me when I would never have believed he could break down his scorn and see past it. He was in a kind of grief, though not able to admit it. His grief matched the truth that he had no place in the world to belong. Ella's Frank helped him get a place in a local barber shop—he learned that trade from his little brother Percy back in Ionia. It was not the farming he had done all his life, but it was a good trade with things that need tending, and people to talk to. No one here knew of his past, and he could have the dignity that he was here to look after me instead of me looking after him.

We knew a few short months of peace together, quietly, not having any significant speech, no apologies. I would talk with him as I fingered my little pinned watch, long since broken beyond repair but still a comfort. Or I would twirl my dry old pen between my fingers as he walked the room or gazed out the window, hands in his pockets.

Then he died, perhaps with mitral valve disease, as his father did. The father and the son so like him both died of broken hearts. When my time comes, perhaps my heart will be a little healed.

Charming little valley,
Smiling all so gaily,
Like an angel's brow,

Spreading out thy treasures,
Calling us to pleasures,
Innocent as thou.

Skies are bright above thee,
Peace & quiet love thee,
Tranquil little dell;

. . .

In thy fragrant bowers,
Giving wreaths of flowers,
Love and friendship dwell.

May our spirits daily,
Be like thee sweet valley,
Tranquil and serene;

Emblems to us given,
Of the vales of Heaven,
Ever bright and green.[26]

[26] verses copied into the opening leaves of the journal, possibly from H.G. Nageli, "Charming Little Valley," in Mason Lowell, *The Hallelujah: A Book for the Service of Song in the House of the Lord . . . to which is Prefixed the Singing School. . . .* (New York: Mason Brothers, 1854), 59. https://books.google.com

AFTERWORD

ROSETTE CORDELIA RAMSDELL CHURCHILL died in December 1914, and records indicate she was buried in Riverside Cemetery, Fargo, North Dakota. No headstone has been recorded as belonging to Rosette, but next to DeWitt Churchill's headstone a taller, thinner stone has toppled on its face.

ACKNOWLEDGE-
MENTS

I HAVE FOUND MYSELF over the years fascinated by books that reveal whole persons by unearthing and sometimes embellishing the primary source materials. Jill Paton Walsh's *Grace*, the novelization of a popular culture heroine of the 1800s, is such a book. Between the lines of newspaper hagiography of this young daughter of an English lighthouse keeper, a girl who one day rescued shipwreck victims, Walsh found in her imagination a young girl overcome by fame. Henry Louis Gates brought to light a novel by a slave woman pen-named Hannah Crafts—*The Bondwoman's Narrative.* Laurel Thatcher Ulrich edited and presented to the world *A Midwife's Tale: The Life of Martha Ballard, Based on Her Diary, 1785-1812.* And in 2015 the world welcomed *Pioneer Girl*, an early autobiographical work of Laura Ingalls Wilder.

Acknowledgements

My grandmother, Ruth Rader Rinaman, created poetry all her life that my aunt, Carolyn Rinaman Durak, collected into a book entitled *Mama's Poems*. In these poems, Grandmom chronicled the signposts of her life. She offered both family history and a personal response, helping us family members know her much better than we might have with just our memories.

For all of these—for my mother, Barbara Carter Day, deceased 2013, who first handed me the junk-store-find journal and said she hoped I would write a book about it; for all who bring to light stories that have not yet been told; for my husband Glenn, who always encourages me to write, and who spirited me away to Rosette's Michigan—I am thankful.

In researching the novel I have had help from many sources, beginning online and extending to meeting with many fine people:

- Jennings Environmental Center, Slippery Rock, Pennsylvania—for my first introduction, in about 2005, to maple harvesting and syrup, since taken up as an occasional family hobby.
- Julie Brittenham Tuttle and the family of William Brittenham, deceased 2008, for their generosity in providing me a copy of his history, *The Garter Family of New York and Michigan.*
- Ford and Evelyn Wright, of Lansing, Michigan, for showing me the sites of Ramsdell and Churchill settlement, and for offering extensive research documents.
- Kathleen Cook, of the Ionia County Historical Society, for offering documents and an enlightening tour of Blanchard House and its museum in Ionia, Michigan.

Acknowledgements

- The ladies at the Lowell Area Historical Museum, for their enthusiasm and research, on the spot, when I visited.
- John and Marie Scheurer, current owners of Jacob Ramsdell's property, for providing hospitality and ownership details.
- The Jeff Badder family, current owners of Otis Churchill's property, for allowing photographs.
- Pamela K. Swiler, of the Ionia County Genealogical Society, and others in that Facebook group, for offering information and interest.
- Connie Norheim, for photographs and research related to the graves of Rosette and DeWitt in Fargo, North Dakota.
- Patti Hobbs, certified genealogist, for sleuthing to improve the accuracy of the history.
- Other writers, friends, and loved ones, for reading all or portions of a draft and offering their reflections and connections.

FOR MORE

*I*F YOU ARE CAPTIVATED BY ROSETTE, as I am, please visit RosetteBook.com to read entries from her journal and notes from my research. Join the Readers List there to receive news and special offers on additional publications, including a transcription of Rosette's journal.

For those who have finished this novel, I want to offer an exclusive, irresistible bonus—Rosette's letters to the women's department of a national magazine in the 1890s, revealing fascinating details of her history and her ideas. I discovered the letters as I was putting final touches on the novel, and they made a delightful difference in the story. Read the real words of Rosette in her sixties and consider the woman she became. Subscribe to the email list After Rosette (awlist4081244@aweber.com) and you'll receive these letters right away and be added to the Readers List mentioned above. Opt out at any time.

Authors depend on the good words of their readers. Please review Rosette on Amazon.com (US and other markets) and Goodreads, or send me a note at info@morainesedgebooks.com. Thank you!

Cindy Rinaman Marsch

96195504R00142

Made in the USA
Middletown, DE
29 October 2018